THIS BOOK
BELONGS TO

_____

GAIL CARSON LEVINE

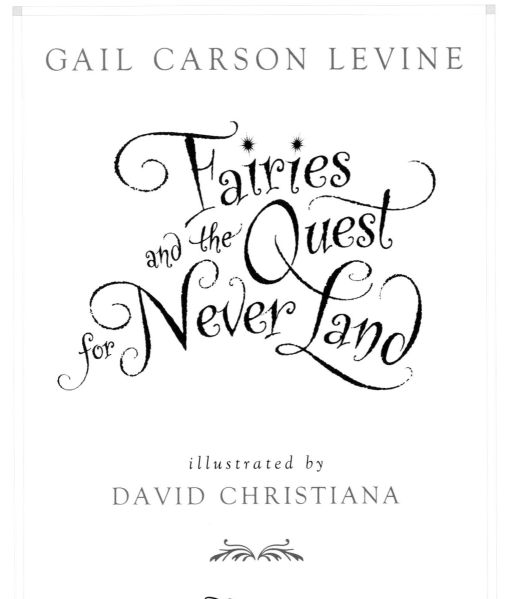

Fairies and the Quest for Never Land

illustrated by

DAVID CHRISTIANA

Disney PRESS
NEW YORK

Text by Gail Carson Levine

Art by David Christiana

Copyright © 2010 Disney Enterprises, Inc.

Library of Congress Cataloging-in-Publication Data on file.

Reinforced binding

ISBN 978-1-4231-0935-8

Printed in the United States of America

First Edition

1 3 5 7 9 10 8 6 4 2

V381-8386-5-10091

VISIT WWW.DISNEYFAIRIES.COM

SUSTAINABLE
FORESTRY
INITIATIVE

Certified Chain of Custody
35% Certified Forests,
65% Certified Fiber Sourcing
www.sfiprogram.org

To Amy and Sean and wedded bliss
—g.c.l.

For Sunny with love
—d.c.

Fairies and the Quest for Never Land

"**G**WENDOLYN Jane Mary Darling Carlisle," Grandma cried, putting down her teacup with trembling fingers, "you are Wendy Darling returned to life."

For her seventh birthday, Gwendolyn had come to breakfast wearing a white dress trimmed with eyelet lace.

"Fetch the scrapbook from my lower bureau drawer, dear," Grandma said. "I want to see."

Gwendolyn returned with a leather scrapbook begun a century before. She set it on the table and opened to the middle, where a girl in a white pinafore stared out at them.

Indeed, the two girls looked very alike: heart-shaped faces, level eyebrows, and serious brown eyes that were trained on something beyond, something unseen by anyone else.

In Gwendolyn's case, she was picturing a five-inch fairy flying over the juice pitcher, trailing sparkles of fairy dust. Gwendolyn inhaled the tiger-lily perfume her grandmother always wore. If I go to Never Land too, she thought, let me meet fairies.

As she blew out her birthday candles, she squeezed her eyes tight and wished, *Peter, come!*

You see, when he remembered, Peter Pan visited the house at Number 14 and brought the latest daughter back to Never Land to do the spring cleaning for him and the Lost Boys. Peter, who was quite behind the times, hadn't yet learned that girls knew boys could clean very well for themselves, at any time of year.

She opened her eyes and saw her father unfastening the silver chain that always hung around her mother's neck.

"The kiss?" Gwendolyn hiccupped, as she often did when she was excited or distressed.

"You're old enough now."

She held her breath as the clasp clicked shut. "I'll take the best care of it."

Of course it wasn't an actual kiss, but an old button made from an acorn. Ignorant Peter had believed it to be a kiss. He'd given it to Wendy soon after they met in the nursery, now Gwendolyn's bedroom. Years later, Wendy's daughter had had the button cast in silver.

Father said, "Every Darling girl has worn the kiss." He blew his nose.

That night, after Gwendolyn's mother read her a fairy tale, Gwendolyn stayed awake as long as she could in case Peter came.

The next night—again no Peter—the kiss felt warm through her fairy-print pajama top. The yellow curtains stirred in a breeze. The window was never completely shut, even in winter, so Peter might enter.

Gwendolyn closed her eyes and heard the roar of surf, although the harbor was almost half a mile away. Had he come?

Her eyes popped open.

No dark silhouette obscured the window. No breath of boy disturbed the air. Only the click of heels against pavement in the street below broke the silence.

She closed her eyes again. . . .

And heard cooing, and saw, on a nest in a hawthorn tree, a dove with glistening white feathers.

Am I dreaming? Gwendolyn wondered.

The dream or vision drew closer. Gwendolyn saw the dove's extraordinary eyes, which were surely filled with feelings and thoughts. Her throat pulsed with the force of her cooing.

"Mother Dove!" someone cried. The voice was breathy, with a ripple of laughter under the words. A glowing figure flew toward the dove, staggering in the air, her arms around a pie almost too big for her to carry.

A fairy?

Excitement brought on Gwendolyn's hiccups. She'd imagined fairies for so long. Don't vanish, she thought, please don't.

The fairy had a tipped-up nose, blue eyes, and red hair tied back in a short braid. She deposited the pie on the nest below Mother Dove's beak. "Dulcie and Tink claim this is the best peach-blueberry pie ever baked."

Tink? Gwendolyn thought. Could she mean Tinker Bell?

Mother Dove pecked the pie. The tip of her beak came up dripping purple juice. "I don't remember when I've tasted such a pie," she cooed. "Beck, tell them how good it is."

Gwendolyn smiled rapturously. This fairy was called Beck. And there was a fairy named Dulcie who might be friends with Tinker Bell . . . Tink.

Beck dabbed Mother Dove's beak with a tiny napkin. The two continued to discuss the pie and the pie tin, which Tink had repaired. This miraculous pie tin would not permit a crust to be either soggy or burnt, and an unjuicy pie was out of the question.

The kiss cooled. The scene faded. Gwendolyn slid into sleep, but in the morning she remembered everything. At school she reenacted every word and gesture to the delight of her friends Carole and Marcia. Marcia judged Gwendolyn's imitation of a bird to be especially good.

The following night, the kiss remained cool, and Gwendolyn didn't see Never Land. Night after night passed, until she thought the vision had been a one-time occurrence. But two months later, in the morning, when she woke up, the kiss was warm.

She heard crashing waves and jingling bells and saw a barn—an ordinary barn—with a steeply sloping roof and a tall cupola, all made of weathered wood. Could this also be Never Land?

The barn came closer. Three mouse faces gazed out from their stalls. The barn door swung open, pushed by a fairy.

Thank you, kiss! Gwendolyn thought.

The fairy was lanky with long, narrow wings. She wore blue coveralls and a cap over straight brown hair.

The mice backed out of sight and reappeared a moment later, trotting out of the barn, followed by five more mice and another fairy. The jingling came from bells tied to the collars of the mice, like cowbells.

Mousebells, Gwendolyn thought.

Over the jingling, she heard her parents' bedroom door creak. Oh, no! Father was coming to wake her up.

The second fairy waved at two more fairies, flying overhead. As the bedroom door opened, Gwendolyn saw that one of the flying fairies wore a tiara.

Might she be a fairy princess? Gwendolyn wondered as her father touched her shoulder.

At breakfast she told Mother about the kiss visions. "Did the kiss show you Never Land, too?"

"Not fairies. Once I saw Peter butted by a deer." Mother laughed. "Peter made finger antlers and butted the deer right back." Her smile faded. "Did you know he hops on one foot when he's trying not to feel sad? I saw him do that in a vision, too, and in real life."

Father spread peanut butter on his toast. "I swear, your mother still has a crush on that Peter."

"Oh, to be young!" Mother said lightly. Peter had come twice for her, when she was eight and when she was nine, then never again.

"When he comes for me, you can say hello to him," Gwendolyn said.

"Better if I don't." Mother put down her toast. "I'd make him uncomfortable. All grown-ups do, unless they're pirates."

Gwendolyn returned to the subject of visions. "Are they real? Did the kiss show you real things?"

Mother hesitated. "It's been many years since the kiss showed me anything. I think what it showed was true, but it may be sending half-truths or lies. Or it may be revealing events of long ago. Who knows?"

TWO

HE KISS visions sometimes revealed aspects of Never Land that had nothing to do with fairies, as when Gwendolyn watched bees defend their honeycomb against a bear, and when she saw a man with elephant-like ears dig under a banana tree.

Grandma said the man was a tiffen. "They're half the size of people. Peter took me to visit their banana farms."

At times Gwendolyn viewed one thing but heard something else. Once, while watching sparrows scratch in the dirt, she heard a fairy named Rani tell Tink and a fairy named Prilla about glimpsing a mermaid named Soop.

Rani's voice had a gurgling sound, like a voice and a brook combined, and she had a habit of finishing the other fairies' sentences. Tink's voice sounded faintly metallic. If a bronze statue could speak, it might sound like Tink. Prilla's voice was lighter and younger than the other two.

Usually, the visions were happy—until one morning when Gwendolyn watched a hawk dive toward a low-flying fairy.

Alerted by instinct, or by the hawk's shadow, the fairy sped up and reached the safety of a bush an instant ahead of the bird's talons. In just a few instants more, Gwendolyn stood at her parents' bedside. She hiccupped twice, caught her breath, then panted loudly on purpose. Father rolled over. Mother smiled in her sleep.

"Can fairies die?"

Mother opened one eye. "Not of old age. Peter said they drown sometimes."

Gwendolyn retreated to bed to think. If fairies could drown, they could also be killed by hawks. Branches could fall on them. A fairy could get stuck in a spiderweb.

She put her hand on the kiss, hoping it would grow warm again and send a more comforting vision. But it seemed to heat up only before or after sleep, and only when it wanted to.

Sometimes the visions offered tantalizing puzzles—a bit of the island here, a bit there, as if Never Land were teasing her. *Here I am! Now I'm gone!*

Luckily, she enjoyed puzzles. Understanding the visions was like piecing a jigsaw puzzle together. When one vision fit with another, she put the two side by side for a bigger view. By the time she turned eight and Peter hadn't yet come, she knew quite a lot about the fairies' home, Fairy Haven, and she had seen or heard more than a dozen fairies.

On her eighth birthday, after Gwendolyn blew out the candles on her cake, Mother said, "Your father and I have been wondering why you like fairies so much."

Gwendolyn sat back in her chair. She just loved them, the way she just loved Mother and Father and Grandma. After a while, she said, "Because they're so small. And I love that every single one has a talent."

"People have talents too," Grandma said. "You solve puzzles that make me dizzy."

Gwendolyn shrugged. She didn't count solving puzzles as a real talent, and fairies seemed too different from her for comparison. They were like living diamonds. Yes, they had faults, but they were perfectly themselves. Vidia, for instance, who was the fastest flier, didn't care about anybody but herself. She was by no means perfect, but she was perfectly Vidia. Fairies were concentrated, like bouillon cubes. That's what Gwendolyn loved most about them, their concentratedness.

Father said, "Your mother tells me fairies aren't interested in humans."

"They call us *Clumsies*," Mother added.

"We *are* Clumsies." Gwendolyn held her plate out for a slice of cake. "We're so big we step on things and bump into things. It's not our fault. But Tink is interested in Peter even though he's a Clumsy."

"Peter is an exception." Mother cut the cake. "The fairies probably won't speak to you, Gwennie, and they may not be pleasant if they do."

Tink had not been pleasant to Wendy.

"I know." But Gwendolyn hoped they would talk to her. She hoped to have a talent for making friends with fairies.

Her spare backpack was always ready and waiting on the floor between her two windows. Inside were a bag of peanuts and dried apples, a canteen of water, binoculars, a toothbrush, and toothpaste. She'd wanted to take a camera, but Mother said photographs taken on the island always came out blank.

Since she was going to be a guest, Gwendolyn decided to bring gifts. She packed a second pair of binoculars for Peter and a sesame-seed bar for Mother Dove. For Rani and the other water-talent fairies, she filled a plastic container with tap water. She was sure they would enjoy foreign water for a change.

For Tink, she chose a tea strainer, only an inch-and-a-half around on a two-inch chain. To make the present even better, she dented the strainer and tore a gash in it. She wanted the damage to give Tink many happy hours of tinkering.

It was hardest to think of a present for Queen Clarion. Finally Gwendolyn found a single earring in Grandma's jewelry box. The earring, a mother-of-pearl disk, glistened pink and blue in a cloud of milky white. Queen Clarion could hang it on a wall or display it in a cabinet, if she liked it.

With the earring in the backpack, wrapped in cotton, nothing was left to do but wait. Gwendolyn calculated the time since Peter's last visit. Twenty years had gone by!

Had he lost all memory of the house at Number 14?

THREE

WHEN GWENDOLYN was eight and a half, her grandmother caught pneumonia. During that terrible time, Gwendolyn had conversations in her mind with Mother Dove, whom she now knew to be the wisest creature on Never Land. She shared her worst fears and imagined Mother Dove's soothing coos.

After a month, Grandma recovered. Gwendolyn thought her thanks to Mother Dove for listening and cooing, albeit in an imaginary way.

On Gwendolyn's ninth birthday, her father asked which fairy she liked best.

"Tink." It had always been Tink—brave, stubborn, adorable Tink.

"Really?" Grandma said, sounding displeased.

Tink had been behind Wendy's near death on Never Land. Out of jealousy over Peter, she had told the Lost Boy Tootles to shoot Wendy out of the sky. Luckily, Tootles' arrow had struck the acorn kiss, thus saving Wendy's life.

Gwendolyn wanted her family to understand. "Even though Tink believes she isn't emotional, she feels more than anyone. If another fairy is in trouble, Tink wants to fix her. If I were in trouble on Never Land, Tink would help me if she could."

One night, when Gwendolyn was nine and a half, the kiss showed a hurricane hitting the island. Trees were bending and cracking. An oak tree flew through the air. In Pirate Cove, waves crested over Captain Hook's pirate ship. Gwendolyn heard thunder and Mother Dove's voice, begging for her egg to be spared. This egg held Never Land's magic, the magic that kept Clumsies and animals there from growing old.

Gwendolyn hiccupped, and, without meaning for them to, her eyes flew open. The kiss cooled. Mother Dove's voice died away. Gwendolyn stayed awake for hours, fretting and wishing the kiss warm again.

Three days passed, and the kiss stayed cool. Each morning, Gwendolyn went to school worried and came home worried. On the fourth day, while she was trying to pay attention to Mrs. Bern's definition of *mirage*, a light pulsed above the teacher's left shoulder.

A fairy! Prilla, who'd been in several kiss visions—freckled, wearing a green beanie and a rose-colored dress—the newest fairy on Never Land. Prilla in person!

The fairy fluttered to the chalkboard and stood on top of

the frame. "Clap to save Never Land!" Her voice was amazingly loud for such a tiny thing. She sounded hoarse, perhaps from urging thousands of other children to clap too.

Gwendolyn led the applause, clapping louder than anyone. From one row back, her best friends Carole and Marcia clapped enthusiastically too.

Mrs. Bern smiled in confusion. Prilla vanished. Gwendolyn excused herself and went to the girls' bathroom, where she clapped for another five minutes.

She pitied Mrs. Bern, who had entirely missed Prilla's presence. Grown-ups couldn't see or hear fairies. Mother said the good parts of being an adult made up for the loss, but Gwendolyn thought everyone should have both.

After school, she relived Prilla's visit again and again, wishing she'd shouted out a question about why Never Land needed saving.

That night the kiss showed her a clear sky over the island, then a dozen fairies lifting a branch away from a tiny door at the bottom of a huge maple tree. One of the fairies was Rani, who no longer had wings. Gwendolyn gasped, but Rani was smiling.

After the vision faded, Gwendolyn mourned Rani's wings and counted it a miracle that fairies had survived the storm.

❀

Months passed without a sign of Peter. In her unhappiest moments Gwendolyn feared he had come already. Number 14 stood in a row of three-story look-alike brownstone houses. If he'd failed to notice the numbers, he might have entered the wrong window and left with the wrong girl.

Her house came next-to-last on the long street that wound its way up from the harbor. On March twenty-first, the day she turned nine and three quarters, she stopped by the wharf after school and stared out to sea.

Unlike the mainland, which stayed put, Never Land roamed the ocean, avoiding ships and map makers, found only when it wanted to be. At this moment it might be just beyond the horizon.

A green bird flew over a sailboat at the entrance to the harbor and then soared into the clouds. Gwendolyn started for home. A quarter of the way up her hill, a long shadow passed overhead.

She looked up. Peter Pan!

She ran. How could he come when she wasn't tucked in bed and ready?

"Wait!" she shouted.

He flew into her bedroom window.

She pounded up the hill, panting. Would he leave when no girl was waiting for him?

The bedroom window closed.

Her chest felt about to explode. As she ran, she fumbled in her skirt pocket for her key.

At last she reached the door, but her hand was shaking so hard she could barely fit the key in. Finally she succeeded and tore up the stairs.

She opened her bedroom door cautiously. Mother stood against the wall between the two windows.

Peter was nowhere, but Gwendolyn heard muffled crying.

Mother pointed at the closet and whispered, "I closed the door and the windows to keep him here. He's crying because I grew up." She smiled wistfully. "I half wish I hadn't."

Gwendolyn hugged her. Poor Mother.

"Two weeks on the island, sweetie. Then come home. Have fun." Mother patted Gwendolyn's cheek and left, closing the bedroom door with a loud click.

Gwendolyn stood in front of her closet, feeling a little afraid. This was it . . . the beginning.

FOUR

GWENDOLYN addressed the closet, saying the traditional words although she no longer heard sobs. "Boy, why are you crying?"

Peter flung the door open and spoke his traditional words, "I never cry." He stepped into the room. "Wendy?"

"Gwendolyn."

"Oh. Gwendolyn. Look! I have my shadow this time." He waved his arm, and his shadow on the floor waved too.

She wondered if this was traditional as well. "It's a lovely shadow," she offered, making her own shadow wave back. She could barely keep from jumping up and down.

"Wendy—"

"Gwendolyn."

"Gwendolyn, do you know any fairy tales?"

"Hundreds!"

He smiled, flashing tiny teeth. Baby teeth? Gwendolyn wondered how old he really was. He was shorter than she was, but Wendy had gone to Never Land a hundred years before.

Fairy dust sparkled as he flew to stand on the bed, which was lumpy with Gwendolyn's crumpled-up pajamas under the blanket.

Her pajamas! She should have been wearing them instead of her school uniform. She was going to be a sight in Never Land in a navy-blue skirt, a maroon blouse, striped socks, and, worst of all, sneakers—the unfairy footwear.

A hiccup started, but she swallowed it back. She was not about to let sneakers kick her out of happiness.

Peter said, "Now I shall sprinkle fairy dust on you."

She shouldered her backpack and reached the bed in two long strides.

From the pocket of his green smock he brought out a tiny sack that couldn't have held more than a quarter teaspoon. "The fairies call this a *daily allotment*." He emptied the sack's contents over her head.

Goosebumps popped up on her scalp before even a speck of dust settled. Then, as soon as the first sprinkle touched her hair, she tingled all over, even between her toes. When the tingling dimmed, she bounced on her heels—and bumped her head on the ceiling.

"Come!" Peter opened the window and flew out.

But she didn't know how. Although she thought, Forward!, she remained butted up against the ceiling like a helium

balloon. The only way she could move was by hand-walking across the ceiling to the window, where she ducked out and stood on the ledge.

Peter flitted above a roof across the way. Separating them, the road spooled out three stories below.

I'll fall! she thought. Her fingers dug into the window frame.

She pushed off and didn't plummet. But after gliding a few feet, she hung in the air, and now there was nothing to push off against. Cars and pedestrians passed below.

Someone might look up! She held her skirt close to her knees. Peter was no longer across the street. "Where are you?"

Hands pressed into her back. She advanced, like a train pushed by a caboose. But Peter couldn't push her all the way to Never Land! She divided the air with her arms as if swimming the breaststroke, which accomplished nothing. She tried scissor-kicking.

"Stop that!"

She went limp and let him shove her to the opposite roof.

"How do you do it?" she asked when they landed.

"I'm clever."

She had been told of his boasting. "Show me, please."

He rocketed into a cloud, then dived out. "Oh, the speed of me!"

"Please show me again."

Obligingly, he did so. He flew without either bending his knees or flapping his arms.

She rose straight up like a window shade, and he had to pull her down. Again and again he showed her. Again and again she failed. Then, when she was sure he was about to give up, she saw him wriggle his shoulders the tiniest bit.

Of course she wriggled far too much, but she flew. "Look at me!" she cried, as her mother once had, and Grandma had, and Great Grandma, all the way back to Wendy, John, and Michael.

Peter zipped away toward the harbor, as graceful as a sea swallow, while Gwendolyn bumbled along. He led her up into the clouds, where she discovered cloud owls.

They surrounded her, each owl the size of her hand with dots of blue sky for eyes. The owls crowded so close she stopped flying and hovered.

(Cloud owls are never seen from airplanes. When a plane passes by, they blend into one another.)

Peter pushed his way through. Afraid she might hurt them, Gwendolyn tried to twist out of their path, but in her awkwardness she hit more than he did. Whenever she collided with one, her wrist or chin or calf felt wet and cold. She shivered. They were like ghosts.

"Am I hurting them?" she asked.

He shrugged. "Dunno. They're just gossips."

What did they gossip about?

"They won't speak while you're here." He took her hand and helped her fly beyond the clouds.

She waved good-bye.

"The Lost Boys will be frightfully glad to see you. They haven't had a mother in ever so long."

Ugh! Gwendolyn's mother had warned her of this. Gwendolyn made her expression stern. "Good. Bedtime at seven every night and no snacks between meals."

Instantly, Peter added, "Of course, you won't be *my* mother."

Below them stretched the open sea, waves and foam to the horizon.

"Fly toward the sun." He zoomed ahead much too fast for her to follow.

"Come back! I'll be a nice mother! I won't be strict!"

His figure shrank to a speck, then vanished.

A hiccup rose into her throat. *Hic! Hic! Hic!* No ships sailed below. No birds soared above or below. Behind her, the mainland had receded to nothing.

The sun set. Gwendolyn continued toward the pink glow on the horizon until it faded. Then she just hoped she was flying straight and concentrated on technique.

If she flapped her arms, she wobbled. If she kicked, she seesawed up and down. She was steadiest keeping her arms at her sides and her legs straight. Moving her hands and feet like flippers increased her speed. Extending one arm or the other made her turn. Lowering or raising her head made her descend or rise.

When she finished experimenting, she pulled the peanuts and dried apples out of her backpack. While she munched, the night brightened with a million more stars than she had ever seen. She rolled over and smiled up at them.

Peter crowed behind her. "You're going the wrong way!"

"Where were you?"

"Ocean mermaids have longer tails than lagoon ones. Listen, Wendy—"

"Gwendolyn."

"This is how to find your way. First look for the Kyto constellation and sight along the dragon's higher wing—"

"What dragon is he?"

"The only dragon on Never Land. Hates everybody. Has the hottest flame of any dragon anywhere."

Gwendolyn's flying faltered. Mother and Grandma hadn't mentioned a dragon. Gwendolyn hoped he lived far from Peter's home and Fairy Haven.

"On land he lives on Torth Mountain. In the stars, his wing leads to the Golden Hawk constellation." He pointed. The tip of the hawk's right claw was a white star, which Peter had named *Peter*.

"Aim for Peter," he said, "and you can't go wrong, unless Never Land moves." He flew away.

Gwendolyn continued on, pleading in her mind with Never Land to stay still. The kiss brushed her arm and warmed the spot. If she closed her eyes she would see the island.

Ah, it was nighttime there, too. Tink hunched over her worktable and picked up a colander.

Never Land faded. Gwendolyn was asleep.

A rush of air woke her.

She was falling headfirst.

A black triangle sliced the waves below.

A shark's fin!

FIVE

A HUGE HEAD thrust up. Jaws opened.

In her fright, Gwendolyn forgot how to fly. She flapped her arms, kicked, and screamed. She flapped harder, kicked harder, screamed louder as she plummeted toward rows of teeth. Rows of swords!

Five feet away.

Aaa!

Three feet!

Two!

Inches from those teeth she raised her head and leveled out, wriggling her shoulders and hiccupping so hard her body shook.

More fins collected in a circle below. Maybe they were friendly sharks who ate only seaweed. Maybe they'd gathered to keep her company.

She flew upward as fast as she could.

Eventually, the stars set, and the sky faded to pale blue before dawn. Gwendolyn breakfasted on the remaining nuts and dried apples. Clouds gathered. She couldn't steer in clouds and could barely fly with the cloud owls pressing against her.

"Wendy, have—"

"Gwendolyn." She exhaled a long breath of relief.

"Gwendolyn, have you ever seen whales dance?"

"No." But she wanted to. "Where?"

"They're finished now. They lift themselves out of the water down to their tails."

"It's over? Why did you tell me if it's over?"

"They dance only for me."

He was infuriating! Maybe seagulls would come and recite poetry in her ears.

He scattered fairy dust on her. "Listen."

She heard nothing more than the waves' *shush-shush* and the wind's *whoosh*. The cloud owls began to drizzle. "What?"

"The pirates are singing."

"Hook's pirates?"

Peter stood straight in the air, grinning. "Aye, Hook's dogs."

She heard a distant *boom*! "What was that?"

"The pirates fire Long Tom every day at noon."

Their cannon? she thought. How many times? She stood up straight, too, pedaling backward.

Luckily, no more blasts followed.

The drizzle ended and the cloud owls drifted away.

A rainbow spanned the sky. On the horizon, midway between each end, was a dot no bigger than Gwendolyn's thumb. She pulled her binoculars out of her backpack and brought them to her eyes.

A brigantine lay at anchor in the bay. Beyond it sparkled a crescent beach rimmed with palm trees. Behind the palms rose a green hillside.

She whispered, "I'm here, really here. Fairies very soon."

They flew over Mermaid Lagoon, where three mermaids were sunning themselves on Marooners' Rock. A breeze rippled through their long hair and trailing scarves. They waved.

Gwendolyn flew lower, waving back. "Hello! You're so beautiful."

But their greeting had been for Peter alone. They dived and splashed. Gwendolyn brushed the droplets off her skirt.

"They're snobs," he said. "You have to have a tail to be somebody to them."

"They like you."

"I'm Peter."

White sand spread below them. Behind the beach, dense forest grew. Gwendolyn's eyes sought a maple tall enough to poke above all the rest. This would be the Home Tree, where the fairies lived.

She followed Peter to the clearing above his underground

home with the Lost Boys. Six faces watched their descent.

Gwendolyn hovered. She hadn't landed since the rooftop on the mainland, when Peter was still holding on to her.

The Lost Boys—Tootles, Nibs, Curly, Slightly, and the Twins, whose names were unknown even to themselves—clustered shyly at the edge of the clearing.

Peter landed. Without looking, he gestured at Gwendolyn's shadow, where he thought she stood. "Your new mother's here. She knows lots of fairy tales and can't wait to scrub and darn for you."

Fortunately for Peter, Gwendolyn didn't hear a word.

Kindhearted Tootles understood her dilemma. "Blow out all the air that's in you."

Gwendolyn did and landed without breaking an ankle. "Thank you." She felt bashful and also embarrassed to be seen in her school uniform. The Lost Boys wore animal skins, which seemed more proper here.

"Hello," she said.

No one spoke.

She racked her brain for polite conversation. "The sea was calm."

No one spoke. Peter had disappeared down the tree hole of an elm.

She tried again, repeating a curious statement she'd heard

at the dinner table, "Only bears are in the market right now."

Slightly nodded wisely. "Indeed. Just bears. No squirrels."

Gwendolyn was surprised by how young the Lost Boys seemed. Nibs, the tallest, came up only to her nose.

"This is the tree for her," Peter announced, emerging from the tree hole. "Wendy—"

"Gwendolyn."

"Gwendolyn, you can go down this tree."

"Down?"

You see, the underground home had seven entrances—one for each Lost Boy plus Peter—but no door. These entrances were holes in seven hollowed-out trees. Each boy got in by sliding down his own hole, which fit him as snugly as a glove.

Gwendolyn stood over the dark hole and felt dizzy.

Tootles said, "You've never seen a home like ours."

Peter looked eager, and even grumpy-looking Curly was almost smiling.

Gwendolyn tucked her skirt around her, lowered one leg and then the other into the hole, until she was seated on the edge. Maybe they had food down there. She was awfully hungry.

She held her arms at her sides and slid. Her waist disappeared into the tree and lodged there. Blushing, she said, "I can't go down any more."

"I'll push you through," Peter said.

How would she get back up? "Don't!"

He was already pressing on her shoulders, forcing her down until he could push no more, and only her head and neck stuck out above the tree hole. Below, her feet dangled, but the rest of her was wedged in.

"I'm coming up." She tried to wriggle though there wasn't room enough. "Pull me! Please."

Nibs tried but couldn't squeeze his hands in.

She would have hiccupped if her chest could have expanded. Was she going to spend her two weeks in Never Land in a tree? At least Tootles, who seemed the most sympathetic, might convince a fairy to visit.

Would she spend the rest of her *life* in a tree? No more school or friends or puzzles or Mother or Father or Grandma. No future, except in a tree.

**"S**HE'S IN my tree." Slightly sounded offended. "Where I will sleep tonight is a mystery, a mystery indeed."

Gwendolyn glared at him. Where she was going to sleep tonight was no mystery at all.

"Don't worry," Peter said. "I'll guard you. The wolves won't eat you."

"Wolves?"

"Big ones," Peter said with evident satisfaction. "Much taller than on the mainland. Never wolves have a double set of teeth, and—"

"Stop!" Gwendolyn's mind went to fairies. What would a fairy do?

Tink would make a metal shoe horn, Clumsy size, to get her out. Prilla would . . . "Clap! Clap to lift me!"

Peter caught on first and clapped with all his strength. The Lost Boys joined in, looking confused. Gwendolyn kicked. The tree groaned, and she flew out.

"We'll whittle a tunnel for you in a new tree," Peter said.

She saw her chance. "While you do, I'll explore." She wanted to be alone when she met the fairies.

Peter looked surprised. "I can show you about later, Wendy."

"Gwendolyn. Er . . . Fairy Haven is that way?" She pointed.

He nodded. "But they—"

"This is for you." She gave him the extra pair of binoculars from her backpack.

He fell back a step, looking uneasy.

"You put your eyes here . . ." She showed him. "Twist this, and you can see things far away."

He still didn't take it. She held the binoculars up to her eyes, which caused a Twin to gasp in fright.

"If you fly above the trees, you can use it to see the deck of the pirate ship."

Peter's hand closed around his present. "See you later."

Warm air nuzzled Gwendolyn's face as she flew. Viewed from above, the trees merged into a green carpet. She couldn't pick out an individual tree or judge its height, so she swerved toward the shore.

A bent stick poked out of the sand. No, it wasn't merely a stick. She landed and dug around it, as delicately as an archaeologist, until she loosened her find, which turned out to be a lute in perfect condition. The fretwork below the strings crisscrossed in a rose-petal pattern. Dark and light woods striped the rounded bottom where tiny holes had been pricked. Why?

To let water drip out. This was a mermaid's lute!

She clapped her sandy hands. What luck! Rani, who loved mermaids, would adore it.

Cradling it in her arms, Gwendolyn flew along the beach and surveyed the forest. In the distance the upper branches of a tree jutted up, topping the surrounding trees.

A shiver ran through her.

Flying inland, she reviewed the little that her kiss visions had shown her of the Home Tree. From fairy chatter, she'd picked up its name and height and that it was a maple. The visions had taken her inside Tink's workshop, with its shiny steel walls and pile of broken pots, and into Rani's bedroom, with the leaky ceiling, the waterbed, and the watered silk

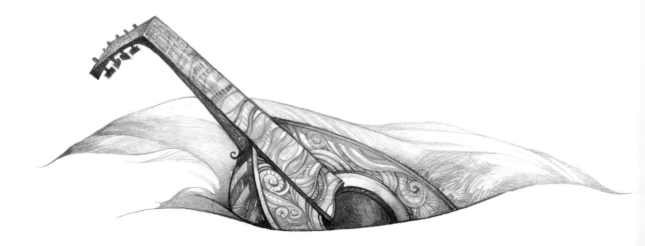

curtains. But she hadn't seen the outside of the tree, except for a partial glimpse of the door at its base.

She drew near and rose a foot out of pure excitement. Maybe a fairy scout was observing her right now.

"I'm a friendly Clumsy," she called.

When she reached the tree, she swooped down, trying not to knock into branches, but knocking into some anyway. She exhaled, came down hard, lost her balance, and tumbled backwards, protecting the precious lute against her chest.

A Clumsy landing, she thought ruefully. Then the importance of the moment overwhelmed her. She sat back, hiccupping softly, and looked up.

SEVEN

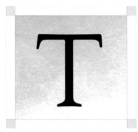

THE MAPLE'S massive trunk rose out of ankle-deep fallen leaves. Its overlapping bark, layer on layer, gave the tree an air of great age. At the bottom was an oval tree knot. Above, the tree's crown of branches and leaves spread wide enough to shelter a crowd of Clumsies or a herd of deer or a magnificence of fairies. No wonder this was the Home Tree.

If it was.

To Gwendolyn's left, columbines bloomed. To her right, a row of white rosebushes led to an oak sapling. She set the lute down carefully, swallowed, and squeaked out the fairy greeting, "Fly with you."

No one answered.

Maybe she'd spoken too softly. "Fly with you."

She heard only the *swish* of a nearby stream. She didn't see even a glimmer of fairy glow or catch a whiff of fairy cooking.

This might not be the Home Tree after all, or perhaps the fairies had gone away.

Or they were shy. She opened her backpack and took out the fairy presents. "Look, Tink! A Clumsy tea strainer for you to fix." It didn't sound like much.

Tink did not appear.

With dwindling hope, Gwendolyn held the other gifts up and announced which fairies they were meant for. Last, she raised the lute. "Rani, here's a mermaid's lute." She strummed it. It twanged like an iron nail across a grating. She plucked it, and the *boy-yoy-yoy-yoinggg* echoed in the woods.

"A mermaid would play better." With desperate cunning, she added, "Rani . . . some mermaid may want it back. The mermaid might be grateful to a fairy who brought it to her."

A squirrel dashed up the oak sapling. A brook burbled. Rani didn't appear. Gwendolyn returned the gifts to the backpack and comforted herself by thinking, I'm on Never soil. I'm here. She patted the trunk of the maple. It was always comforting to touch a tree.

She cast her mind back to her visions. Several times she'd seen a mill on a stream, called Havendish. The mill ground fairy dust from Mother Dove's molted feathers. Gwendolyn had been hearing water since she'd landed.

A short flight over two meadows brought her to a narrow stream. She flew in both directions but failed to spot a tiny mill.

It's a puzzle, she told herself. One strategy for puzzle solving was to do the easy parts first. Finding Mother Dove should be easier than finding a fairy, since Mother Dove was bigger.

Gwendolyn flew higher. From her new perspective, the two meadows were light green thumbprints, the stream a mere pencil line edged by forest. To the west of the stream was another meadow, this one almost an exact circle.

Mother Dove lived in a hawthorn tree on the edge of a place called the fairy circle. In the meadow, a ring of dense blue-green grass sprouted.

Gwendolyn flew lower, her flight wobbling with excitement. Mother Dove would tell her how to find fairies. In fact— Gwendolyn's flying wobbled even more—the fairy Beck might be at the nest right now. She rarely left Mother Dove's side.

Gwendolyn landed in the meadow and turned slowly, shading her eyes from the setting sun and scanning for a hawthorn tree.

There! Bushy, covered with flower buds.

She heard birdsong, but not a single coo. She flew around the hawthorn, although the thorns scratched her face and arms.

"Mother Dove?"

This couldn't be the only hawthorn. She backed into the circle. The trees formed a green wall. Mother Dove's nest might be just a few feet into the forest, but Gwendolyn could spend months finding it. She felt so disappointed she was sure the fairy dust was draining right out of her.

Leaving the circle, she wandered on foot to other maples, none as majestic as the first. She felt so tired she could hardly stand up and so hungry her stomach no longer even rumbled.

Night descended. In the darkness she stumbled over a root, fell, and rolled onto her back. Twinkling above was the star Peter in the Golden Hawk constellation. Her eyes closed. Before she could worry about wolves with double rows of teeth, she was asleep.

An owl hooted. A Never deer nibbled her sneakers. Dawn came. Gwendolyn's first full day on Never Land began. She woke on a single, clear thought: What if, after I left, Rani came out for her lute?

If the lute was gone, fairies had been there. Too keyed up to remember to fly, she ran one way and then another before getting her bearings and racing to the big maple.

The lute was there. She sank down next to it.

Nothing had turned out as she'd imagined. She had pictured her first fairy encounter—the fairies' bashful smiles, her own beaming admiration, and then their joyous welcome. In her dreams she'd pleased them so much that they invited her to spend her entire visit in Fairy Haven.

She gave in and cried. As the tears slowed, she grew angry. It wasn't fair. Mother and Grandma and Wendy had had the Never Land adventures they'd hoped for, but Gwendolyn

wasn't going to. She'd waited and waited, longer than they had, and she wasn't going to.

She picked up the lute. No fairy would ever strum its strings. No Clumsy–fairy friendship would be formed because of it. With all her strength, she hurled the lute at the oak sapling. She missed the skinny trunk, and a *crash* came from the woods.

Leaves rustled. When she looked up a fairy was hurtling at her.

Gwendolyn smiled so widely her cheeks hurt. As her ears drummed and her heart pounded and her stomach flip-flopped and her toes clenched, she thought, A fairy, at last.

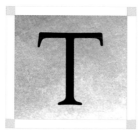HE FAIRY coming at Gwendolyn had a pointy face, long black ponytail, and wings with jagged edges. Could she be Vidia? Gwendolyn recalled her kiss visions. Yes, this was Vidia, the fastest fairy—and the meanest.

She hovered a few inches from Gwendolyn's nose. "Fly with you, darling. Would you throw me, too? Make me go fast. Throw me!"

Gwendolyn opened her mouth, but her breath wouldn't come.

"Dear heart, don't talk. Throw me."

But Gwendolyn wanted more than anything to speak to her first fairy—if only she had air, and words. What should she say? Finally "Hi!" erupted. She blushed. "I mean, Fly with you. I'm so glad you spoke—"

"Sweet, throw—"

A sparrow man—a male fairy—dropped between Vidia and Gwendolyn.

"Fly with you!" Gwendolyn told him. "I'm so happy . . ."

He grabbed Vidia's arm. She wrenched herself free and zipped backwards. He buzzed back and forth, blocking Gwendolyn.

She didn't know which one to help, or how. She seemed only to know how to smile. They were both so brisk in the air, so controlled, so right. Of course Vidia was faster, but the sparrow man had an air of alertness. "Are you a scout?"

He whirled in the air and faced her, eyebrows raised, eyes wide.

Gwendolyn lowered her voice to a whisper, not wanting to frighten him. "I'm so glad to see you."

He flew up into the leaves of the maple.

"Love," Vidia said, "throw me."

"Really? Throw you?"

"Hard, the way you threw the lute."

"Why?"

"To make me fly faster, sweet."

"But you're already the fastest."

"And you're already the least intelligent. One can always go faster, dear."

Wonderful! Gwendolyn thought, if anything, smiling even wider. Vidia was being herself, not worried about insulting the Clumsy.

"I'm waiting, love."

"But I'll hurt you." Still, Gwendolyn held out her right hand, palm up.

Vidia landed, spread her legs for balance, and folded her wings.

It felt like a butterfly had settled on her, except Vidia weighed more than a butterfly. Gwendolyn brought her trembling hand up to the level of her face. "I'm Gwendolyn, and you're Vidia. I know—"

Vidia yawned.

Gwendolyn closed her hand, leaving the fairy's head out at the top and feet out at the bottom. Vidia's wings tickled her palm, and Vidia's glow shone between her fingers. She pictured a fairy's delicate rib cage and tried not to squeeze.

"If you don't hold me tighter, sweet, you won't be able to throw me hard. Don't worry about my wings. They never hurt."

Gwendolyn tried to squeeze and not squeeze at the same time. She wound up and threw overhand as far as she could.

As soon as Gwendolyn let go, Vidia's wings spread and beat the air. Her glow made a line of light, streaking away, slowing, turning, coming back.

"Again, darling."

Gwendolyn watched Vidia's rapt expression as she waited

for the throw. Vidia closed her eyes and mouthed *Go!*

As Gwendolyn threw, she thought, Harder, stronger, farther.

"Again, sweetheart."

Gwendolyn threw again. And again. And again. Vidia wanted no conversation. For her sake, Gwendolyn became a throwing machine, promising herself to keep going as long as she could raise her arm.

When her shoulder began to scream with pain, the sparrow man and two more fairies landed side-by-side on the lowest branch of the maple. One fairy seemed to be another scout, judging by her watchfulness. The newcomer in the middle wore a tiara.

Could it be? Gwendolyn wondered, her pulse racing. Could this be Queen Clarion?

Queenliness was in the lift of the fairy's chin, the directness of her gaze, the purity of her glow, the classic upsweep of her wings.

Gwendolyn curtsied, a very un–Never-fairylike act. "Queen Clarion—"

"Ree. Call me Ree."

"Queen R-Ree, I'm honored."

Vidia lighted on Gwendolyn's hand again.

"That's enough, Vidia," Queen Ree said. "You'll tire her out."

"Tire the Clumsy? Can't be done, Ree darling."

The two scouts flew to Vidia and hovered next to her.

"I'm leaving. Gwendolyn, dear, work on that weak throwing arm."

Gwendolyn felt the tiniest pressure as a heel pushed against her hand. In a moment Vidia vanished into a clump of leaves at the edge of the clearing. The scouts returned to Queen Ree and stood protectively at her side.

"Fairies," Queen Ree announced in a ringing tone, "I believe we are safe. You may leave your hiding places."

Why had they felt unsafe? Gwendolyn wondered. They had seen Clumsies before.

Fairies pushed leaves aside and swarmed around her. She stood stock still, resisting the urge to stand straighter and suck her stomach in.

"No freckles," one said.

Another fairy pronounced, "Brown hair."

"Dimpled chin."

They were discussing Gwendolyn as though she were a new fairy, just blossomed out of a laugh. She felt her heart expand with joy.

"Wide smile," sang a fairy with a beautiful voice.

A singing-talent fairy! Gwendolyn thought.

"Long nose."

"Long feet."

"Long, period."

Gwendolyn pointed at them. "Short, period."

They laughed. She laughed, too, while thinking, I'm laughing along with fairies! She told them her name again, and they started telling her theirs and their talents. She concentrated as she heard each name and talent, knowing she'd never forget a single one.

"Look!" Queen Ree cried.

A new miracle began.

P AND DOWN the maple, in lines and rows along the trunk and the thicker branches, layers of bark rolled back to reveal windows and doors. Fairies appeared at the windows, putting out flowerpots and hanging wind chimes.

Gwendolyn couldn't stifle her excited hiccups. This *was* the Home Tree! This was how it was supposed to look.

But why had the fairies been hiding?

Delicious scents wafted out: pie, stew, bread. If Gwendolyn's empty belly could have spoken, it would have yodeled.

A scout pulled at the knot at the base of the tree, and the knot opened on tiny hinges. It was really a door, the Home Tree's grand entrance. Five fairies wielding brooms exited and flew around Gwendolyn's feet, sweeping up dead leaves. To help, Gwendolyn rose a few inches, while calling, "Fly with you" to each of them.

Below the leaves were pebbles set in whorls and swirls.

Queen Ree perched on Gwendolyn's shoulder, which

Gwendolyn instantly raised to make more level.

"This is our pebbled courtyard," Queen Ree said. "The pebble talents took a year to make it."

Gwendolyn hadn't known there were pebble talents. "I love the way the stones fit together without any spaces."

"We do too. Watch! Over there." Queen Ree pointed.

Beyond the oak sapling, fairies lifted a tangle of vines to reveal the barn Gwendolyn had seen in her second kiss vision. Eight mice waddled out.

Adorable, Gwendolyn thought fondly.

Queen Ree returned to her branch on the Home Tree. Gwendolyn was sorry she'd left, but her shoulder relaxed.

An apple filled the entrance. Gwendolyn's mouth fell open and watered at the same time.

The apple emerged completely, along with three fairies, who were half pushing, half lifting it from behind. They were followed by three more fairies, shouldering a banana, then pairs of fairies, each pair bearing a peach, a plum, and a nectarine.

One of the ones pushing the apple had floury hands and hair dusted with flour. "You must be hungry," she said. "We'll start baking and cooking for you. I'm Dulcie. Here."

Gratefully, Gwendolyn held out her hands. Food at last, and not ordinary, mainland food. This was fairy-grown. "Tha—" Fairies didn't say *Thank you*. "It's very considerate." She stuffed

the peach, the plum, and the nectarine in her skirt pockets and the banana in her shirt pocket. The apple she raised to her mouth.

A single apple would make enough apple sauce for at least twenty fairies. "Can you spare it? I'm not that hungry." She held the apple out, even though she thought she might scream if Dulcie took it away.

"We have an orchard, and the tiffens bring us bananas, more than we need," Dulcie said. "Eat."

Gwendolyn took a dainty bite, embarrassed to open her mouth wide. Her tongue was so big. Her teeth were so big. All the way open, her mouth was half the size of a fairy.

Dulcie laughed. "Eat!"

Gwendolyn did. The apple tasted sweet and tart and juicy. She finished it in five bites and then went on to the rest. Each fruit was perfectly ripe, the peach peachier, the plum plummier, the nectarine nectarinier than any she'd ever eaten. When she finished, she was still hungry, but less so.

Turning cartwheels in the air, a fairy crossed in front of Gwendolyn's eyes. "I remember you. You clapped!" She flew in close and tapped Gwendolyn's chin, as if she were tagging home base in a game of hide-and-seek. "I saw you."

"Prilla?"

"You know me?"

Gwendolyn couldn't resist boasting. "I clapped louder than anyone."

"I heard." Prilla flew to Queen Ree. "Somebody should tell Mother Dove she's a good Clumsy."

Gwendolyn hiccupped so hard her chest hurt. Did Mother Dove think she was bad? "Queen Ree, was everyone hiding from me?"

Queen Ree adjusted her tiara. "Gwendolyn . . ."

She looked so serious! Gwendolyn was afraid to hear her answer. Another painful hiccup erupted.

On the Home Tree's second story, the only metal door in Fairy Haven opened. A fairy flew out. Tink! Gwendolyn double hiccupped, out of distress about being hidden from and out of delight at seeing Tink. "Fly"—*Hiccup!*—"with you, Tink."

Tink flew to Gwendolyn's hand, which was longer than she was, and tugged it upward. With a huge effort, she lugged it over the kiss. "When you start hiccupping," she said, "hold the . . . the . . . pendant."

Perhaps she couldn't say *kiss*. After all, it was the kiss that had saved Wendy from Tink herself.

Gwendolyn folded her hand around it. Her hiccups stopped. Tink had fixed her! As if she were a pot!

"Fly with you." Tink met Gwendolyn's eyes. "Mother Dove said you were dangerous."

"She said Clumsies are dangerous?"

"Just you." Tink flew back indoors. No one else moved. The fairies who had been smiling sobered.

Gwendolyn tightened her grip on the kiss. If Mother Dove thought she was dangerous, maybe she was. "Dangerous to fairies?"

"DO YOU think I'm dangerous?" Gwendolyn asked Queen Ree.

"Mother Dove thinks so."

"Because I'm big?"

"We don't know." Queen Ree adjusted her tiara again. "But Mother Dove may have been wrong. You were kind to Vid—"

"—ia. She *is* dangerous! Look!"

Gwendolyn whirled around to see who had spoken. A dozen fairies flew the smashed mermaid's lute toward her.

Rani, the wingless fairy, rode on top. She mopped her tears with a leafkerchief. "Of course you're dangerous. How could you break a mermaid's lute? A *mermaid's* lute?"

The lute neck hung from the lute body. The body had caved in and the wood had splintered. The strings sagged. One string had been sliced.

Gwendolyn's face reddened and her ears heated up. "I'm sorr—" Hastily, she switched to the fairies' phrase. "I'd fly backwards if I could." If only she could un-throw the lute.

If only she could make herself un-dangerous.

The fairies set the lute down gently.

"I found it on the beach. Rani, I took it for you. I'd fly—"

"—backwards. You said that already." Rani climbed down from the lute. "You took it for me? And then you threw it?"

"I couldn't find any fairies. I thought you'd vanished or gone away. I was angry."

Dulcie said, sounding insulted, "Why would we go away, and how could we vanish?"

More fairies flocked around the lute and examined it inside and out. Rani stepped out of their way. Gwendolyn wondered if they might be stringed-instrument talents.

One said, "We can repair—"

"—it?" Rani said. "You can?"

"Better than ever."

Rani's face turned from sad to happy, although she didn't stop crying. "A real mermaid's lute!" She stroked the wood, then looked up, her glow turning pink. "Esteemed Clumsy Gwendolyn, thank you for the gift."

Esteemed? Thank you? Gwendolyn thought, confused. These were strange words from a fairy.

Rani added, "Esteemed Gwendolyn, I no longer believe you're dangerous."

"Esteemed Rani," Gwendolyn said, "I am grate—"

"—ful." Rani laughed. "Don't call me *esteemed!*"

Gwendolyn turned to the queen. "Queen Ree, can I talk to Mother Dove?"

A chorus of fairies cried, "I'll go with you."

Queen Ree nodded. "If Mother Dove tells you to leave, you have to go."

Gwendolyn held the kiss, and the need to hiccup vanished. "I will." But she wasn't sure she'd be able to.

"Tink!" Queen Ree called.

Tink stood in her doorway, looking grumpy.

"Escort Gwendolyn to Mother Dove."

"I'm busy." But her frown vanished. Fairies loved to visit Mother Dove.

"Take her," Queen Ree said.

Tink streaked away without turning to see if Gwendolyn was following.

"Wait!" Gwendolyn called.

Tink soared back. "What?"

"Queen Ree"—Gwendolyn opened her backpack and took out the presents—"did you hear me talk about these?"

"I did."

"Would you make sure the right fairies get their gifts?" She held up the box that contained the earring. "This is for you."

"That's very kind."

"Tink, this is for you," Gwendolyn said, placing the tea strainer on the pebbles.

Tink landed next to it. "Had a hard life, haven't you, poor thing?" She patted the strainer here and stroked it there, then picked it up in both arms, flew it through her door, and reemerged a moment later. "When do you need it back?"

"It's a gift."

Tink nodded. "Come along." She flew away again.

Gwendolyn picked up her backpack and wriggled her shoulders, but nothing happened. "Queen Ree, I need more fairy dust."

Tink returned and leaned against the oak sapling, arms folded across her chest.

From her kiss visions, Gwendolyn recognized the sparrow man flying toward her. He was Terence, a dust talent who loved Tink, although she didn't seem to love him back.

He took off his beanie and lifted out a fairy-dust sack. At least six sacks had fit in Peter's pocket without making it bulge, but a single one filled Terence's cap. "I'll come along to Mother Dove," he said, while sprinkling on the dust.

Tink set off again. Gwendolyn leaped into the air after her. Terence flew at Gwendolyn's shoulder as they passed over the sapling, the barn, and the two meadows. She descended for a closer look at Havendish Stream.

Terence shouted, "Watch your feet!"

Gwendolyn lifted them and just missed kicking the fairy-dust mill to splinters. She flew higher. My size does make me dangerous, she thought. "Can fairy dust shrink me?"

Tink turned and tugged her bangs. "No, it can't shrink you."

They zigzagged through an orchard and entered the woods beyond. The sun flashed between the trees.

Gwendolyn touched her kiss. Depending on what Mother Dove said, this flight might be her last time with fairies. She flew slower.

Tink was out of sight, but Terence stayed with her.

She tried to start a conversation. "Um, Terence. Um . . ."

He smiled. His smile tilted up on the right. Gwendolyn wondered why Tink didn't care for him.

"I was frightened too," he said, "the first time I met Mother Dove."

Gwendolyn didn't want to talk about the terror of the coming meeting. "Um, Terence . . ." What would he want to discuss? His talent. "Is every grain of fairy dust magical?"

His smile widened, and he slowed even slower than Gwendolyn. "Every grain. If you sliced a grain in half, each half would be magical."

Gwendolyn nodded, glad to hear it.

Tink flew around a pussy willow to come at them from behind. "Mother Dove is waiting!"

Of course this was nonsense, and even Gwendolyn knew it. Mother Dove never left her nest, so she was always waiting.

"Er, Tink . . ." Gwendolyn cast about for a topic. ". . . is there anything you've always wanted to fix but never had the chance?"

Tink was caught, as Terence had been. She hovered, her expression dreamy. "A crinkle slicer. No one has ever brought me one." Her hand made waves in the air. "It has such a shape."

"A crinkle slicer?" Terence said.

Gwendolyn was certain he would find a damaged crinkle slicer somewhere. "Tink, what took the longest to fix?"

"The unleaky colander I have right now"—she zipped ahead but called behind her—"because I keep being interrupted."

Gwendolyn saw a clearing through the trees, the same clearing she'd visited before, which had been the fairy circle all along. Her fairy-dust tingle sparked with fear. Mother Dove's claws held her fate.

A string of coos rippled through the woods, echoing as if a dove were roosting in every bush.

"We moved her nest from the hawthorn," Tink said.

Terence added, "So you wouldn't find it. We'll carry it back soon."

Gwendolyn hardly heard. The coos pounded in her ears. Tink led her toward a dogwood tree.

Mother Dove, let me stay, Gwendolyn thought. She pulled the backpack off and fumbled in it until she found Mother Dove's present. Shouldering the backpack again, she gripped the treat hard.

They neared the tree. There, on a low branch, whiter than the blossoms around her, Mother Dove sat on her nest, her feathers spread over her egg. Gwendolyn's fear faded. She felt peaceful, as she did sometimes when she gazed at the sky from her bedroom window.

The fairy Beck straddled Mother Dove's neck. "Keep your distance, Clumsy."

By rowing backwards with her arms, Gwendolyn stopped in midair a yard from the nest.

"Ree says she's all right," Terence said, as he and Tink landed on Mother Dove's branch.

Thank you, Terence! Gwendolyn thought.

Tink added, "She made Vidia fly faster for almost an hour."

Thank you, Tink!

Beck's glare hardly changed.

"Terence . . ." Gwendolyn held out the present. "Would you give this to Mother Dove? It's a sesame-seed bar."

Terence stretched his arms around the bar and flew it to

the nest, where he set it down by Mother Dove's chest.

"Thank you, Gwen-n-n-dol-l-l-yn-n-n," Mother Dove cooed, without pecking through the wrapping to taste it. "Why have you come to Fairy Haven? Most Clumsies stay with Peter."

"Because I love fairies, and I always have. They say you think I'm dangerous. Maybe I am. I could squash a fairy by accident." She choked out a laugh. "Ten fairies."

Beck's glare softened.

Mother Dove said nothing.

"Is that it? Will I squash a fairy?" Gwendolyn didn't know if Mother Dove could see the future.

Mother Dove cooed and cocked her head from side to side again and again. Gwendolyn went on hovering. Mother Dove was evaluating her, she was sure, in what might be the most important test of her life.

Tink said, "I have this unleaky colander . . ."

Mother Dove went on cooing.

Gwendolyn sat on a branch of a beech tree across from the dogwood.

At last Mother Dove stopped cooing. "Gwendolyn, I fear you love fairies too much. You will have to stay away from Fairy Haven."

ELEVEN

"OH!" TERENCE said, sounding shocked.

Along with despair, an undertow of resentment pulled at Gwendolyn. Yes, she loved fairies, but she also loved her parents and Grandma. Could she love them too much? Could she love anything she loved too much?

Surprisingly, Beck chimed in with the same question. "Could I love you too much, Mother Dove?"

"Yes, Beck."

"Then why don't you banish me?"

Mother Dove cooed. "You're my companion. I could love you too much too. But I help you, and you help me."

This isn't right! Gwendolyn thought.

"It isn't fair." Hands on her hips, Tink hovered in front of Mother Dove. "How will she hurt fairies?"

A thrill ran through Gwendolyn. Tink was defending her!

Mother Dove shook her head. "I can't put my claw on it."

Tink returned to the branch.

"Could she help fairies?" Terence asked.

Mother Dove cooed an even longer string than before. She shifted in the nest, revealing a curve of egg. Suddenly she squawked.

Gwendolyn almost fell off her branch. Beck gasped. Tink's wings fluttered. Terence's glow darkened.

Mother Dove returned to cooing.

At last the coos ended. "Trouble is coming to Never Land. I can't see what it will be, but kindness will cause it."

"Will I cause it?" Gwendolyn blurted. "By loving fairies too much?"

"Gwen-n-n-dol-l-l-yn-n-n, the trouble won't come from you."

"When it comes, I want to help."

Mother Dove's gaze rested on Gwendolyn's face. Gwendolyn felt a feather stroke her cheek. But no feather was near her. "I can't tell if you will help or harm fairies and Never Land. You may be of great help, but beware of yourself."

Gwendolyn nodded. She would try not to hurt a fairy, but she couldn't love them less. Then the full meaning of Mother Dove's words reached her. "I can stay?"

Mother Dove smiled. "Matters have changed, and we will take the chance. You may stay."

Terence cried, "Hooray!"

Mother Dove pecked through the wrapper and nibbled at the sesame-seed bar. "Delicious. From the mainland?"

"From Little Moon Street near—"

"Look!" Beck cried. "A Plum Paula!" She rose above the nest and pointed down toward the fairy circle. "Mother Dove, may—"

"Go ahead. I'll have a word with Gwendolyn."

Gwendolyn felt uneasy as Beck, Tink, and Terence flew off.

But Mother Dove only asked, "Your grandmother is better now, isn't she?"

"Grandma? You know Grandma had pneumonia?"

"I follow Wendy's line. Is she well now?"

"She's fine." Gwendolyn blushed. "I talked to you while she was sick, to help her get better. Did you help?"

Coos were Mother Dove's only answer.

In the fairy circle, Beck was dancing, hand-over-hand, leg-over-leg, with a butterfly almost her size. Nearby, Terence smiled and Tink swayed in place.

Gwendolyn wondered how they could be carefree if trouble was on its way.

"The trouble will come soon enough," Mother Dove said as if reading Gwendolyn's mind. "Why fret now?"

Gwendolyn nodded. "Is that the Plum Paula?"

"Beck says it's the largest butterfly on the island."

Below, Beck and the Plum Paula backed away from each other, came together, then backed away again.

"I could watch forever," Gwendolyn said.

Terence jumped between the butterfly and Beck to join the dance.

"I wish I really could," Gwendolyn added, thinking ahead to the day when she would lose fairy sight.

Beck and Terence and the Plum Paula circled Tink, who was clapping time. Gwendolyn thought Tink's expression a trifle impatient.

Mother Dove said, "Many years ago, Never Land made me extraordinary. I don't know why it picked me." Her coo sounded like a chuckle. "The island has its whims. If it wants to, it can let you see and hear fairies for as long as you live."

Gwendolyn snapped her head up. "It can? The island?"

"If it wants to."

Gwendolyn wondered what she could do to help it want to.

"Gwen-n-n-dol-l-l-yn-n-n, Never Land can't be persuaded or forced to do a thing. It does what it likes."

Oh. Still, this was astonishing news. She flew down to the fairy circle where Beck, Terence, Tink, and the Plum Paula were spinning above the grass, aerial tops that crossed and recrossed. On her own, Gwendolyn whirled and twirled, too. She might see fairies forever. Mother Dove had said it.

She collapsed on the ground, laughing. When she sat up, she saw that the Plum Paula had gone, and the fairies had returned to the nest. She went back to her branch.

Mother Dove pecked a spot on her own shoulder. "Beck, I have an itch. Would you . . ."

Beck thrust her arm deep into Mother Dove's feathers. "Is that it?"

"You always find the—"

"My unleaky colander. I need . . ."

As fast as a falling coconut, Peter plunged past everyone yet still landed softly. "We whittled a tree for you, Wendy."

"Gwendolyn."

Tink scooted along the branch until leaves hid her. Terence stood up.

"Wendy, I meant *Gwendolyn*. I mean, Gwendolyn, I meant *Gwendolyn*."

Tink slipped back out from the leaves. Her glow was scarlet. "Fly with you, Peter."

"Hullo, Tink."

"This is my friend Terence."

"Fly with you," Terence said.

"My good friend Terence." She slid next to him.

Peter hopped on one foot. "Wen—Gwendolyn, you can come to the underground home now." He flew above the treetops.

She owed him a visit, and they'd whittled out a whole tree for her.

But if trouble was looming, should she leave?

Why fret? she thought, remembering Mother Dove's words. She launched herself. Looking down, she called, "I'll be back soon, and I'll *beware*."

Gwendolyn and Peter landed in Peter's clearing. The Lost Boys were there, each shouldering a rough fishing pole.

"We're going to fish in the lagoon, Wendy."

"Gwendolyn." Obviously she wasn't invited.

"Gwendolyn. This is your tree. I'll go down, too." Peter led her to a walnut tree, then stepped into his own tree hole in a white birch and was gone.

Feeling nervous, Gwendolyn peered into her tree. The smell of mold drifted out. Swallowing her fear she stepped in and hovered. Yes, it was big enough. She exhaled.

Her stomach seemed to drop quicker than she did, like in an elevator. She landed on soft wood shavings and stepped out

of her tree. Dim light filtered down through the tree holes.

"Come." Peter took her hand and brought her to the sink, a blocky shape in the dark. "Soap is underneath. Pail too. The mop is leaning against the sink. Here . . ." He tugged her a little to the right. ". . . is the water pump." His voice was proud. "Goes right into the sink. You put your hands here." He placed them. "And press down hard."

She pressed.

Distant gurgles sounded, followed by clanks. Water spurted, stopped, spurted, then gushed.

"You've got it. Now this . . ." He raised something she dimly perceived as a basket. ". . . is your darning."

The smell of dirty socks overwhelmed the odor of mold. She pinched her nose.

"Wendy loved her darning, Gwendolyn." He disappeared up his tree and called down from above, "Have a rollicking good time."

TWELVE

WENDOLYN squinted into the murk. The home was a single room, half filled by a bed and one quarter filled by a tabletop balanced on a tree stump. Tree trunks lined one wall, brown, naturally, except for Peter's birch, which gleamed the ivory of an old bone. Packed earth made up the other walls, the ceiling, and the floor, where mushrooms grew—tiny brown mushrooms, huge red ones, and medium-sized purple ones.

A cupboard leaned against the wall next to the bed. She opened a door—and shut it instantly. Whatever food was in there was crawling with ants.

She considered flying right back up her tree. Then she saw it—the only pretty spot in the room, a nook in the wall across from the sink. She had forgotten about this nook, although she'd heard of it in family stories. It was *the* nook, Tink's bedroom, her boudoir, as she used to call it. She'd lived in it when Wendy came, while Tink still regarded herself as Peter's fairy.

Gwendolyn longed to go to it but wouldn't let herself. The

nook would be her reward. Because of it she would stay and work.

She decided to start by making the bed. But a beetle scrambled across the bed sheets. Horrified, she backed away into the tabletop. She could wash the dishes.

Dirty plates were so stuck to smeared honey and dried gravy and who-knew-what-else that she could hardly pry them up. Her stomach flopped queasily.

After a struggle, she loosened the dishes and carried them to the sink. Under it she found Pirate Ship-Shape soap flakes with a picture on the box of bo'sun Smee cleaning his spectacles. She began to scour. Pretending to feel cheerful and not revolted, she whistled while she worked.

Her fingers were pruny by the time the dishes were as clean as she could scrub them. Since there was no hygienic place to put them, she stacked them in the sink. Next, she carried the pail filled with soapy water to the table and began to rub. In five minutes the sponge turned so black it wouldn't rinse back to yellow.

She gave up, feeling she had earned her prize.

Tink's nook was the size of Gwendolyn's head. The walls, floor, and ceiling were hammered brass that must have shone when Tink lived here. With a fairy inside, glowing, a Clumsy would have had to shade her eyes.

Tink had been gone for decades. The night table tilted on

off-kilter legs. A cobweb hung between the carved bedposts and the tiddlywinks chandelier. Gwendolyn pulled the cobweb away with a finger, then maneuvered her hands in to remove the rugs and the couch cushions. She snapped a finger against each one to beat out the dust. With a single feather from the Lost Boys' feather duster, she swept the floor and dusted the chest of drawers.

There. What an elegant place it was.

How wonderful it would be to have a souvenir of Never Land.

It wouldn't be stealing, Gwendolyn told herself. Nobody lived in this cranny now. Its beauty was certainly wasted on Peter and the Lost Boys. Besides, she wouldn't take much, just the rugs and the chandelier. When she got home she could make a fairy room to put them in.

Carefully, she rolled the chandelier up in the carpets and tied the bundle with thread from the sewing kit in the socks basket.

She paused with her booty halfway in the backpack. Mother Dove had said *Beware*.

What if the rugs and the chandelier had to be here in the coming trouble?

Carpets? A lighting fixture? Not likely.

But what if?

Gwendolyn returned them, although she couldn't remember which way the rugs had been facing. If the trouble required them to be the right way, she had already failed.

Outside, the sun was setting. The air smelled sweet. Gwendolyn put out her tongue. If only she could eat air.

No need, because when she reached the Home Tree, a feast had been laid out in the courtyard. Surprisingly, the bowls and plates and portions were almost Clumsy size. Gwendolyn hovered and inhaled the spicy, lemony, and sweet scents.

Dulcie flew to her. "See? We can feed a Clumsy. When the tiffens come we bake and cook for them." She wrinkled her nose. "They won't eat anything that doesn't have bananas in it. It was more of a joy to make things for you."

Gwendolyn landed on grass at the edge of the courtyard. Fairies stood between the dishes. She sat gingerly, making certain she wasn't crushing anyone. The silverware was smaller than she was accustomed to, but usable. The stems were silver bananas.

Six fairies flew a bowl of pink liquid to her.

"Cream of raspberry soup," Dulcie said.

"Isn't anyone else going to eat?"

"We had dinner," three fairies said at once.

Gwendolyn swallowed a gulp of soup while everyone watched. "Mmm. Delicious."

Every single fairy said, "Ah," in satisfied voices. Then most flew into the Home Tree. Only Dulcie and Marla, a cook, remained. Marla stood next to the pepper mill, which was almost as tall as she was. Dulcie perched on Gwendolyn's calf, halfway between her skirt hem and the top of her sock. As soon as she landed, Gwendolyn was more aware of the dots of skin beneath Dulcie's feet than of any other part of herself.

"Try the bread," Dulcie said.

"Try the noodles," Marla said.

Gwendolyn tried both, both delectable, everything delectable, even the baked okra. Cooked by fairies, she thought. Cooked *for me* by fairies.

While she ate a slice of banana cream pie, fairies holding unlit lanterns flew out of the barn and hung them on the oak sapling. Could these be light-talent fairies? All but one flew into the Home Tree. The remaining fairy went from lantern to lantern, rapping each in turn with her knuckles. Every time—*pouf!*—a lantern flared. When all were lit, the fairy waved to Gwendolyn as she entered the Home Tree.

"Oooh," Gwendolyn breathed. "Tiny stars in the tree."

The lights made the courtyard a bright bubble. Every pebble gleamed. The white columbines glistened, and the roses seemed to radiate from within.

Dulcie said, "Sometimes we have midnight picnics out here."

Gwendolyn swallowed her last bite of pie. She put down her plate and patted her lips with her napkin. She had rarely felt so relaxed. "You know," she said, "the second-best part of being here is the food."

Marla frowned. "What's the best part?"

"Fairies."

Dulcie and Marla smiled.

Feeling bold, Gwendolyn began, "Do you think . . . Do you . . ." She took a deep breath. "Do you like me?"

Dulcie said, "You're a good eater. We like good eaters."

Gwendolyn's heart pounded. What if a fairy came home with her? Even without Tink's chandelier and carpets, Gwendolyn could make a tiny home. A real fairy would be a million times more fun to play with than dolls. "My mother and father are good eaters too. You could cook or bake for us at home. Would one of you want to come with me when I leave? You could both come. Our kitchen is . . ." She trailed off as the two fairies zipped into the Home Tree.

Dulcie appeared in the doorway. She yelled, as if Gwendolyn were deaf, "Fairies practice our talents here. We live in Fairy Haven with Mother Dove."

Gwendolyn's stomach churned. "I didn't mean to insult you."

Dulcie waved her hand at the dishes. "Don't clear up. The stacking talents and the table-to-kitchen talents want to do it." She popped back indoors and then reemerged an instant later. "Clumsies can't understand." She disappeared again and didn't return.

 WASN'T *beware!* Gwendolyn thought. She wondered how long Dulcie and Marla would stay mad. She didn't know if fairies were forgiving or if they held a grudge forever.

Fairy glow shone in the Home Tree windows as fairies sparkled around their rooms, entertaining guests or getting ready for bed.

Would the fairies mind if she slumped down here, or should she slink into the forest?

Poor me, she thought. Even skunks had dens to sleep in.

Of course there was Peter's underground home, but a skunk's den would be comfier.

Tink flew out her workshop door. She flashed in front of Gwendolyn's face, looking annoyed. Gwendolyn concluded Dulcie or Marla had told Tink and the other fairies what she'd said.

"Follow me." Tink darted to the sapling, took a lantern, and left the courtyard.

Gwendolyn, thinking *beware*, didn't dare take a lantern too, so she bumped and scraped as she followed Tink into the woods. Leaves rustled behind her. She turned to see fairy glow and another lantern bobbing along. It was Terence, watching out for Tink.

They flew along Havendish Stream. Gwendolyn feared she was being banished from Fairy Haven.

A weeping willow took shape ahead. Tink flew between the trailing branches and came back out again. Her expression had switched from irritated to merry. "Come in."

Puzzled, Gwendolyn parted the branches. "Oh!"

It was a bedroom! Tink's glow and her lantern lit the green walls and made the leaves shine. The carpet was soft moss. Near the trunk the branches curved high enough that Gwendolyn didn't have to stoop.

The bed, a quilt-covered mound, was exactly Gwendolyn's size. She borrowed Terence's lantern to see the quilt better. Each square depicted a different fairy activity—cooking, baking, milking dairy mice, grinding fairy dust, and so on.

Where had the fairies found enough cloth to make such a big quilt? She pulled a corner aside to uncover a yellow-and-blue striped sheet and a matching pillow case. Beneath the sheet was sweet-smelling hay.

She cried, "Oh, Tink! Oh, Terence!"

Tink dimpled, because the room was delightful or because she'd fixed Gwendolyn again or for some other Tinkish reason. "The quilt and sheet are made from old balloon-carrier balloon cloth."

Terence explained, "We move things in balloon carriers. They're baskets held up by fairy-dust balloons."

"The decor talents got the room ready for you," Tink added. "They want you to know it's called a bower although it has nothing to do with bowing."

"Everything is beautiful." Gwendolyn remembered a kiss vision. "Tink, my bower is like the big roasting pan you turned into a pudding mold."

Tink smiled again. "You know about that?"

She smiled at something I said! Gwendolyn thought. "I do." She told Terence, "The pan was ruined until Tink touched it."

He said, "Tink can do anything."

"Terence! No, I can't."

"My bower was just space under a tree." Gwendolyn felt happy, when she'd been miserable a few minutes before. "Now look at it."

Across from the bed was a chair made of branches twisted and tied together.

Gwendolyn didn't think it could bear her weight, but she pressed down on the seat and it didn't break. Holding her breath, she eased into it and found herself in the most comfortable chair ever.

She stood again to go to the night table. Across the top, fairy silhouettes had been stenciled in gold paint.

Tink said, "The decors made the table from a shed that collapsed."

A tumbler and a porcelain pitcher full of water sat on the table. Of course the pitcher handle was a porcelain banana. Gwendolyn poured water into the tumbler and sipped. "Ice cold." Fairies didn't leave out a single detail.

Terence smiled. Tink fluttered her wings and gazed at the wall of leaves.

Gwendolyn shook her head, marveling. "My own fairy room! Made by real fairies! Er, not that there are fake fairies. Would you tell the decors I love it?"

"They'll be relieved," Tink said. "They didn't know what would be right for a Clumsy."

"Can I give you some water?" Gwendolyn held out the tumbler.

Tink said, "It's late."

Gwendolyn didn't want them to go. "Did you fix the unleaky colander?"

Tink frowned. "Not yet."

"You will," Gwendolyn and Terence said at the same time.

Tink said, "Dulcie told me to say they'll make breakfast for you but not to ask that question again . . . whatever question it was."

So Dulcie and Marla hadn't told.

"Tink . . . after breakfast, can I watch you work?"

She tugged her bangs. "Watch Terence."

"You can watch me. You may have a talent for fairy dust."

Gwendolyn nodded, although she particularly wanted to see the colander leak its first drip and possibly see Tink's dimples again.

Before leaving, Tink and Terence hung their lanterns on the willow branches, since their fairy glow would show them the way home.

Gwendolyn called, "Fly with you," and stuck her head out to watch them go.

Just as they flickered out, a new light sparked up. Gwendolyn stepped outside and watched the glow grow into Dulcie, who was struggling to fly with a saucer of leftover banana cream pie.

Gwendolyn hoped the visit meant she was forgiven. She took the plate and parted the branches for Dulcie to enter.

"I thought you might get hungry again." Dulcie didn't sound angry.

"I am." Gwendolyn took a bite. "It's even better now."

"Fairy leftovers are tasty, and fairy dust keeps food fresh a long time."

Gwendolyn finished.

"Fairies lick their plates when they like their food."

Gwendolyn licked.

"Then nobody has to wash them."

Gwendolyn's mouth opened in an astonished O.

Dulcie laughed until she was gasping for breath. "You believed me!"

Gwendolyn laughed too, not as hard as Dulcie.

"Fly with you." Dulcie took the plate and left.

In bed, Gwendolyn had never felt so comfortable. She drifted off, thinking, Two weeks of fairies. Maybe, before she left, she'd be brave enough to tell Tink that she was her favorite. And after she went home, maybe she'd have fairy sight for the rest of her life.

She woke early, with her hand wrapped around the kiss, which was warm. A kiss vision, here on Never Land!

She heard boyish voices, but not Peter's or the Lost Boys'.

A mountain rose in the distance, then zoomed in closer.

Two tiffen boys knelt on a rocky shelf above a cave. Behind them, a gnarled tree sent its roots over the cave mouth to chew into the rock beneath, imprisoning a dragon—the real Kyto, not the constellation, the dragon who hated everyone, whose fire was hotter than any other. He strained against his tree-root bars.

One tiffen was prying up a root with a knife, while the other boy tugged at the same root.

Wait! Stop! Gwendolyn thought. Don't!

All the roots were giving way. Kyto's cruel face was gleeful. Soon he'd be free!

FOURTEEN

GWENDOLYN dressed with trembling fingers that could barely button a button or zip a zipper. As she left her bower and flew over Havendish Stream she thought of going straight to Mother Dove or Queen Ree, but she didn't want to bother them if this was nothing. Maybe she had misunderstood her vision. Tiffens might often visit Kyto to play this strange game with his bars.

Or the tiffens might be setting off the coming trouble.

Tink would know.

The sun was rising as Gwendolyn rapped a fingernail on the metal door. Tink took a minute to answer. She opened the door while tying on the belt of a silvery dressing gown. Her ponytail was down. Her glow was so low Gwendolyn could barely see it.

"Tiffens are trying to free Kyto!"

She yawned. "How do you know?"

"The kiss showed me."

Tink's gaze sharpened. "Did you tell Mother Dove?"

"I didn't want to wake her."

Tink's expression said, *Stupid Clumsy.*

Gwendolyn hiccupped. "I'll tell her." She flew off.

Tink called, "I'll come right away."

Gwendolyn lost a few minutes, because Mother Dove had been moved back to her hawthorn. When she found her, Mother Dove's head was tucked under her wing. Beck was snuggled into her side.

"Mother Dove!" Gwendolyn hovered in front of her.

She raised her head and blinked sleepily.

"Tiffens are freeing Kyto!"

The sleepy look vanished. She cocked her head. "Yes. Those fools!"

Gwendolyn dropped several inches. This *was* the trouble! "Beck—"

Beck stood erect on the nest. "Yes, Mother Dove?"

"Get Prilla. Hurry!"

Beck was gone.

"How do you know about the tiffens and Kyto?"

Gwendolyn sat on a branch of a neighboring hemlock and told Mother Dove about her kiss visions.

"Please have a vision now and tell me if Kyto is free."

Gwendolyn explained why she couldn't. "And I don't see

whatever I want, and sometimes I hear one thing and see something else. I can't pick."

"I understand." Mother Dove fluffed up her shoulder feathers and lowered her head into them. She made a worried *gug gug* sound in her throat.

While they waited for Beck and Prilla, Gwendolyn wished for the tiffens' knife to be dull, Kyto weak, the tree roots strong.

Mother Dove spoke from deep in her shoulder feathers. "How long ago did you see the tiffens?"

"When I woke up. Maybe half an hour ago. I left my bower and flew to Tink. She told me to come to you." Gwendolyn remembered. "She said she'd come soon."

"You went to Tink and not to me?" Mother Dove extended her neck straight out.

For a second Gwendolyn thought Mother Dove was going to fly over and peck her.

"You wasted time!" Mother Dove's voice was so harsh the hawthorn's leaves rattled.

Gwendolyn swallowed over a lump in her throat. "I didn't realize. I didn't think."

Prilla and Beck flew in and landed on the nest, on either side of Mother Dove. Tink, Terence, and Queen Ree perched on Mother Dove's branch.

"Pr-ril-la . . ." Mother Dove peeped the *p* and rolled the *r* and *ls*. ". . . two tiffens are with Kyto. Would you blink to them?"

Blink? Gwendolyn wondered.

"Tell them they must not loosen his bars." Mother Dove shifted on the egg. "They must not!"

Prilla's wings stilled. "How can I blink to tiffens?"

"They're young," Mother Dove said. "Tiffen children."

Prilla closed her eyes, then half opened them. Her face went blank. Her mouth fell open. Gwendolyn wondered why, then understood. This was a *blink*. Prilla was right there, in front of them, but she was elsewhere in a blink, too!

She snapped her mouth closed. "I was at a zoo. I'll try—" Her head sagged sideways onto her shoulder.

She was back. In the next three tries she said she visited a skating rink, a library, and the bedroom of her laugher, Sara Quirtle.

"Prilla . . ." Mother Dove cooed, ". . . rub my feathers."

Magic lived in Mother Dove's feathers, whether ground into fairy dust or not. Leaning into them, Prilla turned around and around. Her eyeballs rolled back behind her eyelids. Mother Dove steadied her with a wing.

Prilla vanished for a second—or less—or not at all— Gwendolyn wasn't sure. Now here she was again, below the

fairies and Mother Dove, holding two young tiffens by their flat ears. The tiffens wobbled on the ground. Prilla let their ears go, and they fell to their knees.

"Kyto's free!" Prilla yelled. "He was singing!"

Gwendolyn gasped. Where would Kyto go first? How soon would he come here?

The tiffens' skin was scarlet from Kyto's heat. When they saw Mother Dove their faces turned almost purple. One looked at his feet. The other met Mother Dove's gaze.

She cooed, not sounding angry at all. "What are your names?"

The one who met her eyes said, "Arli."

The one who went on looking at his feet muttered, "Tammo."

Queen Ree said, "Why did you set Kyto free?"

"We didn't mean to," Arli said. "He told us he had a cramp in his leg. We felt sorry for him."

Gwendolyn shivered, remembering Mother Dove's prediction: *Kindness will cause it.*

Tammo added, "He said it was his 639th birthday."

"We were loosening a root so he could stretch, when all the roots went *sproing!*"

"What was he singing?" Tink asked.

Prilla imitated Kyto's raspy voice,

"Happy birthday to me.
I'm so hungry, you see.
Sweet young tiffens for dinner,
Happy birthday to me."

Tammo said, "As he was breaking free, he said he wanted to crisp fairies most of all."

Gwendolyn gripped her branch to keep from falling.

FIFTEEN

GWENDOLYN looked up fearfully, half expecting to see a dragon shape growing in the western sky.

"We want to stop him," Arli said.

Gwendolyn saw Tammo notice her, stare, then turn away.

Mother Dove cooed. "Arli and Tammo, hurry home. Your part will be to tell your parents. Tiffens must prepare. Kyto will be weak at first, but not for long."

Tammo started to leave, but Arli stood his ground. "Tiffens don't do anything except debate. Not Tammo and me. Most tiffens."

"Then be safe with them while they debate," Mother Dove said, "and try to persuade them to get ready."

The tiffens left, Arli walking backwards as if he were thinking of more arguments.

"Er," Gwendolyn began, hoping Mother Dove was still speaking to her, "are you going to ask Peter to help?"

At *Peter*, Tink moved closer to Terence.

Gwendolyn wasn't sure if Peter would be a reliable ally. When he was winning a fight, he sometimes switched sides to keep the battle going. Still, he was bigger than fairies, and he fought pirates.

"No," Mother Dove said. "Peter will kill Kyto or get himself killed. I don't want either of them to die."

"But Kyto is evil," Prilla said.

Queen Ree answered. "He's part of the island."

"Gwen-n-n-dol-l-l-yn-n-n," Mother Dove cooed, "fly home."

"You said I might help!" Or harm.

"Your mother and your grandmother expect you back safely."

Gwendolyn shook her head so vigorously that her hair whipped around her face. "If they were here, Mother and Grandma would stay. Wendy, John, and Michael would have stayed. I'm staying."

Mother Dove raised and lowered her wings in defeat. "When fairies meet Kyto, do what Ree or Tink tells you."

"I will," Gwendolyn said solemnly. "I promise."

Queen Ree said, "No questions, and you'll have to be quick."

"Yes, Queen Ree."

Prilla asked, "Can we give Kyto more items to put in his hoard, so he won't hurt Never Land?"

Terence explained for Gwendolyn. "Kyto's hoard means the world to him. Tink and Prilla and Vidia gave him things for it once before."

Tink said, "But now he can take whatever he wants."

Mother Dove stood up in her nest and flapped her wings, which frightened Gwendolyn as much as anything else. Didn't Mother Dove always remain on her egg?

Beck hovered in front of Mother Dove's face. "Maybe I could—"

"No, Beck." Mother Dove settled back down. "A dragon isn't an ordinary animal. If you entered his mind, he might swallow you from the inside."

Gwendolyn imagined Kyto's mind as flaming pointy teeth.

"What if he had other things to think about when Beck went in?" Queen Ree asked. "What if he were distracted?"

Mother Dove cocked her head. "Maybe. Beck, fetch Rani."

Beck started for the Home Tree.

"Wait!"

She flew back.

"I want Vidia too."

"Vidia?" Beck said, sounding shocked.

"Vidia."

Beck headed off again.

"Bring Moth too," Mother Dove called, "and a few scouts."

Beck caught a swell of air and hung.

"Tell everyone to come."

Gwendolyn imagined Beck delivering the news. Fairies in their workshops would look up as they listened, their projects forgotten. Sewing talents would accidentally cut cloth instead of thread. Carpenter talents would hammer their thumbs. Fear would spread from Beck to other animal talents to the creatures of Never Land.

Fear everywhere, fanning out like dragon fire.

SIXTEEN

"COULD CLAPPING help?" Prilla asked, then went blank again, so Gwendolyn knew she was blinking. "Mother Dove . . ." Her voice faltered. "We'll be no more trouble to Kyto than a mosquito to a Clumsy."

What had Prilla seen to say that? To diminish her own fear, Gwendolyn said, "A mosquito can drive me crazy."

Apparently cheered up, Prilla did a handstand on the nest. "*We'll* drive him crazy."

Fairies began arriving, landing on Mother Dove's hawthorn or in the fairy circle. Vidia perched three branches above Gwendolyn in the hemlock.

Rani flew in on the back of another dove. She patted the bird's head and jumped onto the branch with Terence and Tink. "Fly with you, Brother Dove."

Brother Dove flew down to the clearing.

"Mother Dove, why did you send for us?" Dulcie asked. "Beck wouldn't say a word."

"Kyto has gotten free."

Gwendolyn thought the sun had gone behind a cloud, but it was really fairy glow dying out for a moment.

Mother Dove added, "Captivity weakened him, but he'll regain his strength quickly."

Rani wept into a leafkerchief. The rest of the water talents cried too. There were no other tears. Fairies were brave.

Queen Ree straightened her tiara. Terence's hand hung an eighth of an inch from Tink's shoulder. The hand didn't pat her, but it didn't move away either.

Mother Dove said, "Tink will design a new cage, and all the pots-and-pans talents will build it."

Tink's glow flared. Then her wings drooped. "We may not have enough metal."

Mother Dove cooed, which Gwendolyn was sure meant, *You will think of something.* "As soon as he gets used to flying again, Kyto will come to Fairy Haven. We must stop him before then. The cage must be taken to him."

Prilla did a split in the air. "It will be a new quest. The quest to cage Kyto."

"Rani," Mother Dove said, "find a way to douse Kyto's—"

"—flame." Rani nodded. "What way?"

Mother Dove cooed again. "The other talents will plan how to distract Kyto while Tink cages him."

"Are we all going?" Terence asked.

Gwendolyn wanted to go, although her stomach seemed to drop when she pictured Kyto.

"I'll decide who goes," Queen Ree said.

Mother Dove said, "Those who remain will build up our final defenses."

Gwendolyn hated the sound of *final*.

"Vid-d-d-dia . . ." Mother Dove cooed.

Vidia flew up to Mother Dove's nest. "You want my speed, don't you, darling?"

"Go to Kyto, Vid-d-d-dia. See how weak he is. See if he's flying. Come straight back and tell me."

Vidia took off, but before she rose above the hawthorn, Mother Dove cooed, "Vid-d-d-dia . . ."

Vidia zipped back. "Yes, darling?"

"Vid-d-d-dia . . . No matter what you do, I love you."

"Yes, love." In a wink she was a dot over the fairy circle, then nothing.

Fairies gathered in groups by talent. Rani called Prilla to plan with the water talents. No one asked for Gwendolyn, who felt left out, although she thought the clusters of glow beautiful.

"Mother Dove," she said, "how could Kyto hurt fairies?" She couldn't bring herself to say *kill*. "Doesn't he love pretty things? Doesn't he collect them in his hoard?"

Mother Dove just cooed.

"Can I do anything to prepare?"

"Tell me if you see Kyto again in your visions. And you especially need to *beware* now."

Gwendolyn nodded, but she doubted herself. *Bewareness* had failed her twice.

Talent by talent, the fairies left the fairy circle and the hawthorn. Brother Dove carried Rani.

Gwendolyn's fairy dust had run out, so she walked. Lonesome me, she thought, fearsome dragon. She sat on a fallen log and stared down at her lap. There was no hurry. No one would care when she showed up at the Home Tree. If only she were part of Mother Dove's plan and had preparations to make, too.

Fairy glow near the ground caught her eye. Fairies were herding caterpillars. She supposed this was normal until she saw that the caterpillars were being driven out of Fairy Haven. The herding talents were making sure that caterpillars would survive even if Fairy Haven was destroyed. But what would they do without their fairies?

She brushed away a tear and stood. Maybe someone at the Home Tree had something for her to do. If not, she'd prune the rosebushes, weed around the columbines, sweep the courtyard— so everything would be perfect when Kyto came.

Beware! She mustn't even think that.

When she reached Havendish Stream, Prilla and Rani were sitting on the bank, dangling their legs in the water. Brother Dove pecked the ground nearby. Prilla smiled up at Gwendolyn.

"Can I sit with you?"

Prilla nodded.

"You've been crying!" Rani held up a leafkerchief, big enough for a single tear.

"I'm okay now." Gwendolyn wiped her eyes with the back of her hand. She shrugged off her backpack, removed her socks and sneakers, and sat, extending her legs into the water. Her toes popped up halfway across.

Prilla said, "Rani is trying to figure out how to douse Kyto's flame no matter where he—"

"—is. We have to get water to him, but there are no rivers near his cave. And he could be anywhere by now anyway."

They looked hopefully at Gwendolyn.

Fire trucks would be useful, but fairies didn't have them. "What about a hose that you could take with you to Kyto?"

"What's a hose?" Prilla asked.

"A long, rubbery straw."

"Straw?" Rani blew her nose. "As in hay?"

"A hose is long and hollow."

"We don't have any," Prilla said.

"Rani-bat says . . ." Rani's voice lost its expression and

turned mechanical. "'Pardon me, esteemed fairy, but you can't bring water to a dragon.'" Rani's voice became itself again. "Sometimes I wish . . ." She shrugged.

Was Rani-bat another fairy, Rani's twin with a strange vocabulary? "Er . . ." Gwendolyn said, hoping Rani wouldn't mind the question, "who is Rani-bat?"

Prilla said, "Rani has a little bat who lives in—"

"—my head. She's very polite." Rani's glow turned pink. "She tells me to say things."

Now Gwendolyn understood why Rani had said *pardon me* and *esteemed*. But she didn't understand anything else. A real bat? How had it gotten in there? She felt it would be rude to ask, since Rani hadn't explained. Instead, she said, "Could you force water up from under—"

"—ground? We can if there's water a few inches down, but not more. Rani-bat says I should find a cave to hide in and never come out."

Gwendolyn didn't like Rani-bat.

Prilla patted Rani's back.

Rani shook her head, scattering tears. "If only we could sweat and weep enough to put out his flame."

If only I could, Gwendolyn thought. Her sweat and teardrops were bigger.

Prilla jumped up. "Rani, you're thinking like a—"

"—bat." Rani nodded. "I am." She cupped her hand in the stream and lifted it out.

The water stayed in Rani's hand, quivering like gelatin. Gwendolyn stared, then dipped her own hand in and took it out. The water ran through her fingers.

"Think like a fairy," Rani said. "Think like a fairy."

The water in Rani's hand separated into beads so tiny Gwendolyn could barely see them. "Oooh!"

Rani smiled. "Gwendolyn's never seen me use my talent." The beads rolled around her palm without merging. She moved her hand in a circle and the beads arranged themselves in a circle on her palm.

"Oh, Rani!" Gwendolyn cried.

The circle closed in, then widened. In. Out. The beads formed a five-pointed star. Rani bounced the star up and down, and it never broke apart.

Prilla was bouncing too, on the bank.

"I've got it! I know what we can do. Watch." Rani made a fist, opened it, and the water became a single drop again. She tossed the drop into the air.

Midair, it turned into a water bird! Gwendolyn fumbled in the backpack for her binoculars, but before she could bring them to her eyes, the water bird rose through the leaves above her head.

"We can fly the water to Kyto, bird by bird."

Gwendolyn peered through the binoculars, watching the leaves. The bird reappeared, spiraling down. It was a minuscule, see-through hawk, a hawk in every detail: hooked beak, talons, wide wings.

It made a water landing, and merged into the Havendish.

Prilla turned a cartwheel.

"Rani-bat says it's the ideal solution. I have to tell everyone."

Gwendolyn understood Rani meant the other water talents. She watched Rani fly away on Brother Dove. After doing a handstand on Gwendolyn's shoulder, Prilla flew off too. Gwendolyn followed on foot. In a million years she wouldn't have thought of water birds. Maybe fairy ingenuity and fairy artistry could overcome a dragon.

Maybe.

SEVENTEEN

HE MILL was on the way back to the Home Tree.

Gwendolyn heard voices coming from inside. "I've used up my dust," she announced to the air.

Terence flew out. "We're packing enough dust to last for days when we go to Kyto." He poured a daily allotment on her.

The usual tingle thrummed with fright. "*Days* fighting Kyto?"

"Best to be prepared." He smiled his lopsided smile. "Too much beats none at all."

A dust-talent proverb, Gwendolyn thought. "Can I watch the packing?"

He nodded, so she knelt and put her eye to a window. In the mill, fairy dust flowed from a chute at the bottom of each pumpkin canister into canvas sacks held by waiting dust talents. Not a speck of dust escaped.

Terence stood next to her ear. "If Ree picks Tink to go to Kyto, I'm going too, whether I'm supposed to or not."

"If she stays, you stay?"

"No. Not if Ree wants me."

Gwendolyn raised herself into a crouch. "Are you scared?"

"Yes, I am." He twisted the empty dust sack in his hands. "But it doesn't matter if he crisps some of us as long as we cage him."

It did matter! It mattered if he crisped a single fairy!

From the direction of the Home Tree an uproar erupted, sounding like musicians torturing their instruments and singers ruining their voices.

"What's that?" Gwendolyn shouted.

Terence shook his head. "Dunno." He went back into the mill.

"Fly with you!" Gwendolyn yelled, putting her hands over her ears.

In the dairy mice's far pasture an orchestra was going full blast, playing *yawk yeeech gugrug dzzoing kriyiyike* while other fairies screeched *yerk eyetch eee zjjang blayayabe*. The orchestra conductor waved her arms wildly.

Could this be true music, Gwendolyn wondered, and the mainland version just noise?

She landed near the strings and tried to appreciate. After two or three minutes, the conductor lowered her arms. The pandemonium died down. Near Gwendolyn's right sneaker toe, a violinist rosined her bow.

Gwendolyn knelt. "Practicing for a performance?"

The violinist answered with a you-are-a-crazy-Clumsy look.

"No?" Gwendolyn said, blushing.

"We're practicing to make so much noise Kyto can't think."

Their racket might drive him to a quieter island, Gwendolyn thought. She left the musicians and continued on to the Home Tree.

Although it was mid-afternoon, breakfast was waiting for her in the courtyard. The food must have been sitting for hours, but the biscuits had stayed warm and the butter cold. The eggs were still runny, the way she liked them. How had the cooking talents known? She giggled. She must look like a runny-yolks kind of Clumsy.

In the distance the musicians and singers started up again. As she bit into the last toast triangle, two fairies lugged bedsprings through the Home Tree door and left them by the rose bush.

The two were followed by a fairy with her arms full of silver and gold picture frames. She dropped them on top of the bedsprings.

Everything is metal, Gwendolyn thought. It's all for Tink's new cage.

She smelled cooking, with spicy and sweet scents jumbled together.

More fairies carried metal furnishings out. Others brought tools from the barn. A mound grew of fairy-sized rakes, hoes, pails, shovels. Three fairies hauled sacks out of the Home Tree and emptied them on the mound. Eensy glinting sprinkles splashed out, too small for Clumsy eyesight, so Gwendolyn used her binoculars.

The sprinkles were safety pins, straight pins, needles, snaps, and hooks and eyes.

Queen Ree and Rani staggered out of the Home Tree with a bedframe. Queen Ree struggled to carry a lamp as well.

Gwendolyn crouched by them. "Can I help?"

They dropped the bedframe and stood back.

Gwendolyn picked it up. It weighed about as much as her binoculars. Queen Ree pointed up at the top of the mound.

Gwendolyn put the bedframe there. "They're for the cage, right?"

"Tink says it's not going to be a cage." Queen Ree set the lamp down. "Because he already escaped from a cage."

"Then what will it—"

"—be?" Rani dabbed her eyes. "She hasn't told anyone."

Queen Ree said, "The cooking talents and the baking talents are making whatever they can before they give up their pots—"

"—and pans. Everything will taste salty."

"Why?" Gwendolyn asked.

Rani blew her nose.

Oh. Tears were salty. Without cookware, baking talents and cooking talents couldn't practice their talents. Pots-and-pans talents couldn't either. A Never fairy deprived of her talent would hardly feel like herself.

Queen Ree touched the lamp at her side. "The decor talents were going to put this in a shoe talent's room today."

The lamp pole rested on four booted iron feet.

"When is Tink going to use these—"

"—treasures? She's in her workshop, designing."

Queen Ree and Rani returned to the Home Tree for more metal to sacrifice. Gwendolyn flew high above Fairy Haven to see what other preparations were under way.

The dairy mice's near pasture had been scattered with sheets, tablecloths, curtains, split-open balloon-carrier balloons, carpets, and bits almost too tiny to see.

In the air below Gwendolyn, a fairy hollered out directions. On the ground, fairies picked up pieces of cloth and put them down where they were told.

It was a colossal jigsaw puzzle! As she hovered, Gwendolyn kept guessing where the next piece would go, and after a few minutes she knew. The cloth was being laid out in the shape of two dragons, the feet of one pointed toward the Home

Tree, the feet of the other pointed the opposite way. The two lined up at their spines. Sections were missing, but fairies—sewing talents?—began to stitch up the pieces that already fit together.

Hmm. If everything was connected, one dragon could be folded over the other, stitched up partway, filled with cotton or foam, to make an enormous stuffed dragon.

What use could a stuffed dragon be?

Carrying brushes and buckets of paint, fairies glided from

the Home Tree. They landed on the cloth and started painting. Were these art talents?

In quick strokes a fairy painted triangles of light blue-green. Following her, another fairy gave each triangle a shadow of darker green. The paint concealed the seams between swatches of cloth.

After four triangles Gwendolyn knew what she was seeing: scales! Scales that looked sharp enough to rip your skin if you touched them.

With Prilla at her side, a fairy dabbed paint from a wooden palette onto one of the dragon faces. In minutes, sunken cheeks and a wrinkled snout appeared. Prilla gestured at the face.

Gwendolyn descended to listen.

"The expression isn't wicked enough," said Prilla, who seemed to be an authority. "Make the mouth curl down more. Good. Now you've got it."

Even the flaring scales above the eye looked cruel. Gwendolyn fought an impulse to hide from those half-open eyes, which seemed to follow her. Instead, she knelt by a sparrow man who stood at the edge of a dragon belly. "I have some cloth," she began. "If there isn't enough, you can have the quilt and the sheet in my bower."

He smiled. "That's kind, but we've got enough. Keep your sheet and comforter. The decors will be glad you have them."

"Do you mind my asking? What's the stuffed dragon for?"

"Stuffed?" He looked bewildered. "Stuffed? Oh, I see. I suppose it will be stuffed—with dairy talents."

"Why?"

"Because they volunteered."

Gwendolyn felt thickheaded. "Why will they be inside?"

He spoke slowly and extra clearly. "The dairy talents have to keep the dragon suit aloft and help it fly. Speed will come from the fast fliers, who will flap the wings."

"It will fly?" Could she help? Push it from behind?

"When Kyto sees another dragon, he'll go to it. The suit will land in the right spot for Tink. We think Kyto will land too, because he'll want to know where the stranger came from and the size of its hoard."

"What if Kyto isn't flying yet?"

"If he isn't, the suit will land near him and distract him from Tink."

Gwendolyn nodded, impressed by the plan's ingenuity and grandeur. What courage the dairy talents and the fast fliers had, to face Kyto first.

The sun set. Gwendolyn left the pasture although fairies were continuing to sew or paint by their glow light. Periodically the musicians and singers ripped apart the quiet of the night.

In bed, she imagined Kyto flaming at a fairy and felt her own knees and elbows go weak. She was frightened for herself, too, but only in the way she was frightened of a horror movie. Despite what Mother Dove had said, she didn't believe anything bad could really happen to her here. Logically she understood that if Kyto roasted her, she'd die and never go home. But that was just logic. In her belly and her heart she believed that if Kyto's fire raged at her, she would pop up unharmed in the house at Number 14.

The kiss felt warm when she woke up the next morning. She kept her eyes closed.

Kyto was sitting on his hind legs on a ledge midway between his cave and the plains. Gwendolyn's pulse galloped. He might have flown there. He might be flying!

Wait . . . Could this be the dragon suit and not Kyto?

No, because last night less than half the suit had been sewn.

Her vision drew closer.

Vidia stood on Kyto's claw!

Leave, Vidia! Fly—quick! He'll crisp you!

Don't die!

EIGHTEEN

"D ARLING . . ." Vidia didn't sound terrified, and her *darling* didn't ring as sarcastic as usual, or sarcastic at all. "Mustn't arch your back. Fast fliers fly with a flat back."

"Little crispiness, did I arch my back?" Kyto's voice was hoarse and crackly, like a talking fireplace, but the feeling in it was molasses and honey. He was flirting!

"Try again, sweet." She flew above his head.

He faced away from the mountain, pushed off with his back claws, and flew, staying close to the ledge, his back level. He flapped his wings too fast and too hard. His flight was bumpy, but it was flight.

In her bower, Gwendolyn gasped.

He landed two dragon-lengths farther down the mountain, panting out clouds of smoke.

Vidia hovered above the smoke. "Longer strokes with your wings next time, love."

She was teaching him to fly again!

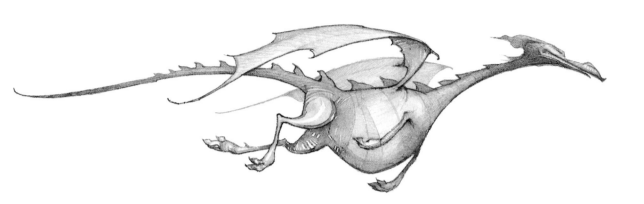

How dared she?

He finally caught his breath. "Show me, precious pearl."

"Watch the wings." Vidia flew back and forth near his face. She hovered. "See, sweet?"

"I see that you are my shooting star, my flaming arrow."

Vidia's glow pinkened. "My turn, dear heart." She fluttered within six inches of his mouth.

He would swallow her!

His chest expanded. His cheeks puffed out.

Gwendolyn dug her fingers into her thighs. He was going to flame!

But he blew a stream of white smoke. Gwendolyn heard a *whoosh* mixed with the high notes of Vidia's laughter. She was using Kyto's breath to fly faster!

When his chest stopped expanding, he inhaled and pulled her back. Gwendolyn heard more shrieks of laughter.

Vidia was an evil traitor who could get other fairies killed. Gwendolyn hiccupped and opened her eyes. She buttoned her blouse wrong at first and jammed her right foot into her left sneaker.

At the nest, Beck was urging Mother Dove to eat an almond pie. Gwendolyn landed in the hemlock and panted out her vision.

"Kyto in flight," Mother Dove said, "is bad news. But thank you, Gwendolyn."

Why isn't she angry at Vidia? Gwendolyn wondered.

"Beck, see how Tink is coming along. I promise to eat my breakfast while you're gone."

Beck hovered. "Mother Dove, why would Vidia help him?"

Mother Dove cooed. "She has fallen in love."

"With Kyto?" Gwendolyn asked, stunned, although she'd seen enough to believe.

"With Kyto. Her loyalty has become divided."

She's still a traitor, Gwendolyn thought.

"Is he in love with her?" Beck asked.

"It is possible."

"Does Vidia . . ." Beck took a deep breath. "Does Vidia still love you, Mother Dove?"

"She is still a Never fairy."

Gwendolyn said, "Has Kyto stopped hating fairies?"

Beck waited.

"He may hate fairies more than ever. His nature is jealous."

Beck left.

Mother Dove pecked at her breakfast. "Gwendolyn, would you eat this for me? I'd like Beck to think I have an appetite."

So Mother Dove was distressed. Although she had no appetite either, Gwendolyn started on the pie, which was about the size of her hand. When she'd eaten a quarter of it, she saw Beck's glow through the trees and crammed the rest into her mouth.

Beck reported that Tink had finished her design and was calling her contraption the Kyto Keeper. She was in the Home Tree courtyard, starting to make it.

Gwendolyn left the nest. If Tink was outdoors, anyone could watch.

Tink sat by the columbines with a muffin tin in her lap. Under the rosebushes, a dozen or more other fairies, probably pots-and-pans talents too, chose items from the mound of metal and flattened them with mallets.

Gwendolyn recognized a familiar shape atop the mound, the tea strainer she'd brought from home. She landed carefully and picked it up. Tink had smoothed out the dent and had repaired the hole so cleverly that Gwendolyn couldn't tell where it had been. What's more, she had added a feature, a layer of mesh to press the tea for extra flavor.

Now her innovation would be destroyed. Why, everything in the mound was probably equally original.

Still, here was something Gwendolyn could help with. She could flatten the pieces much faster than fairies could. Without the slightest inkling of *beware*, she filled her hands with bedsprings, shovels, rakes, kettles, skillets, whatever, and spread everything on the courtyard pebbles. Then she leaped up and stamped down hard.

Someone shrieked.

NINETEEN

AS KYTO coming? Gwendolyn looked up and saw only blue sky. She looked down. Horrified fairy faces stared at her.

Oh, no! She'd done something wrong again. But what?

Tink flew at her, right at her, and stopped an inch from her nose. "Don't do that again."

"Isn't everything supposed to be crushed?"

Tink tugged her bangs and flew to the ground where she picked up what had been a bucket. "We spread them out first, then flatten them. You can't do it haphazard."

"I'd fly backwards if I could." Gwendolyn held her kiss. Why did she always forget *beware* when she most needed to remember? "Can they be fixed?"

No one answered. Fairies descended on the trampled metal. Tink returned to the muffin tin.

Cursing herself for a Clumsy bungler, Gwendolyn stood at the edge of the courtyard. Fairies pulled apart the mess she'd created. If only one of them would say she hadn't ruined the

Kyto Keeper or set work back for days . . . but no one did.

After watching the other pots-and-pans talents for a few minutes, she circled Tink on foot and stopped three feet behind her, hoping not to be sent away.

Using her shears, Tink cut the cups out of the muffin tin. Her tools lay in front of her in neat rows. Rather than step closer, Gwendolyn used her binoculars to see them. Some were familiar: saws, hammers, wrenches. But what was that long-handled, square-headed thing with tiny spikes all over? Or the doohickey like a copper spider with rollers at the ends of its legs? Or the long, narrow curl that could have been an apple peel if it weren't made of metal?

Terence, who stood at Tink's side, called, "Gwendolyn, do you have any spare metal?"

Her skirt zipper was metal, but her skirt would fall down. The zippers on her backpack were plastic.

The kiss! The kiss and chain would be a lot of metal, as much as bedsprings. She reached for the clasp, then hesitated. When Tink flattened the silver, she might harm the precious acorn button inside, the real kiss.

Beware! Gwendolyn thought. Don't be selfish. She cupped her hand over the pendant. Fly with you, kiss.

But without it, she'd lose its visions and the glimpses of Kyto. A rush of relief ran through her. How delightful to have a good reason to keep her kiss!

Tink could have the chain, though. Gwendolyn slipped the pendant into her skirt pocket. She stepped forward and deposited the chain next to Tink. "Here." The chain equaled at least half a set of bedsprings. Gwendolyn's neck felt strange without it.

Tink didn't look up, but Terence said, "Good for you, Gwendolyn."

She wondered if she had more to give. Yes! Metal rims circled the shoelace holes in her sneakers. Each rim was big enough for a fairy bracelet, and there were twenty of them. She could remove the rims and still lace up her sneakers.

She approached the mound again. Fairies looked up in alarm.

"I'm not going to hurt anything!" She found a tiffen knife for cutting out the rims. Gathering her courage, she sat as near Tink as she dared, just a few inches away, then unlaced and took off her left sneaker. She stabbed the cloth around a rim. After a struggle, she yanked the rim out and dropped it into a pleat of her skirt. She looked over to see how Tink was doing. Her shadow fell on Tink, who scowled upward. Gwendolyn straightened instantly.

The glow in Tink's hand intensified as she threaded the apple-peel thingamabob in and out of a strip of muffin tin.

"It's a slit maker!" Gwendolyn said.

Tink dimpled up at her.

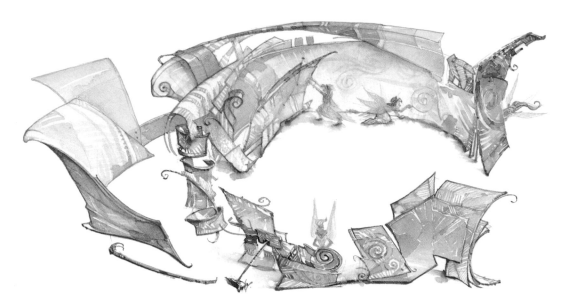

"What are you making?"

"The Kyto Keeper collar."

Terence chimed in. "Which will stay around Kyto's neck forever."

Tink wove another strip of muffin tin through the slits she'd just cut. Her hand's glow or something in Tink herself made the tin as pliable as cloth. She murmured, "There! Gooood! Perrrfect!" The tin whistled as it wove in and out.

For the first time, Gwendolyn felt part of Fairy Haven, really part of it, a Clumsy helping with a fairy project. It was such a precious feeling she sensed herself growing warm, as if she were glowing too.

To her amazement, Tink, fairy of few words, started explaining. "The Kyto Keeper collar has to be stronger than Kyto." She picked up a length of flattened iron. "I'll wind this cut-up pail and a few lamp stands around the tin to make the collar thick enough."

"Won't the sharp edges chafe his skin?" Gwendolyn asked.

"I wouldn't let them chafe!"

Gwendolyn blushed.

Tink trimmed the iron. "The collar will be hinged, like a door. It will open so wide he won't feel it until it claps shut."

Terence chuckled. "He'll be surprised."

"And the collar will be beautiful. It has to be beautiful!" Tink sounded as if someone might disagree. "Gwendolyn . . ." She looked up from her shears.

Until now Tink hadn't ever said *Gwendolyn*. Never before, Gwendolyn thought, has my name tinkled like chimes.

". . . if Peter ever asks you about the Kyto Keeper, will you tell him how beautiful it is?"

Was Tink saying she didn't expect to live to have another conversation with Peter? Gwendolyn gulped. "I'll tell him."

Tink went on. "Three screws will hold the collar closed. They'll go in at the back of his neck where he can't reach."

"That will make him mad," Terence said, sounding gleeful.

Tink added, "He'll strain against the collar with all his might. If the screws hold, Never Land will be . . . If they give out . . ."

Gwendolyn nicked her thumb. If the screws gave out, the island would be a charred ruin.

"THE SCREWS will hold," Terence said. "Of course they will."

Gwendolyn sucked on her cut. "What will the collar be attached to?"

Terence answered, "A chain with a big screw at the end, which will be sunk into a boulder, which will keep Kyto from flying."

"I'll need you to carry the boulder to him," Tink said.

Gwendolyn nodded enthusiastically. She was going on the quest! "What boulder? Where is it?"

"On Torth," Terence said, "or on the plains around the mountain."

"How will I lift it?"

"Fairies will help you," Tink said, "everyone who can be spared. Ree will see to that."

But the strongest sparrow man could barely lift two pounds.

"I'll sprinkle fairy dust on the boulder," Terence said, "and extra dust on you and your helpers."

Gwendolyn wished she had a talent for boulders. Maybe a boulder could be lifted with fairy dust, but what if it couldn't?

She finished taking the rims out of her sneakers and scooped them up. When she piled them next to Tink, who was sitting, they reached higher than the fairy's waist.

Tink picked up one rim. "Copper," she said. "Nice."

Gwendolyn grinned. "*Tha*—good."

Tink spent the rest of the day making the collar. Gwendolyn spent the rest of the day watching. The hinges alone took three hours.

Dulcie and several serving talents flew out of the Home Tree with baskets of cookies.

Gwendolyn checked the sky. "Exactly how far away is Kyto's mountain?"

"Depends," Terence said. "Depends on whether Never Land is big or small."

"I see." But she didn't.

Dulcie deposited a basket of cookies in Gwendolyn's lap. "We'll bring more. Oatmeal-quince-cinnamon, my recipe." She added, "Most times, it takes almost a full day to fly to Torth."

Gwendolyn emptied the basket onto her palm and licked the cookies off. More food was brought out, all cooked or baked before the destruction of the pots and pans.

Tink stood back from the collar. "Done," she said.

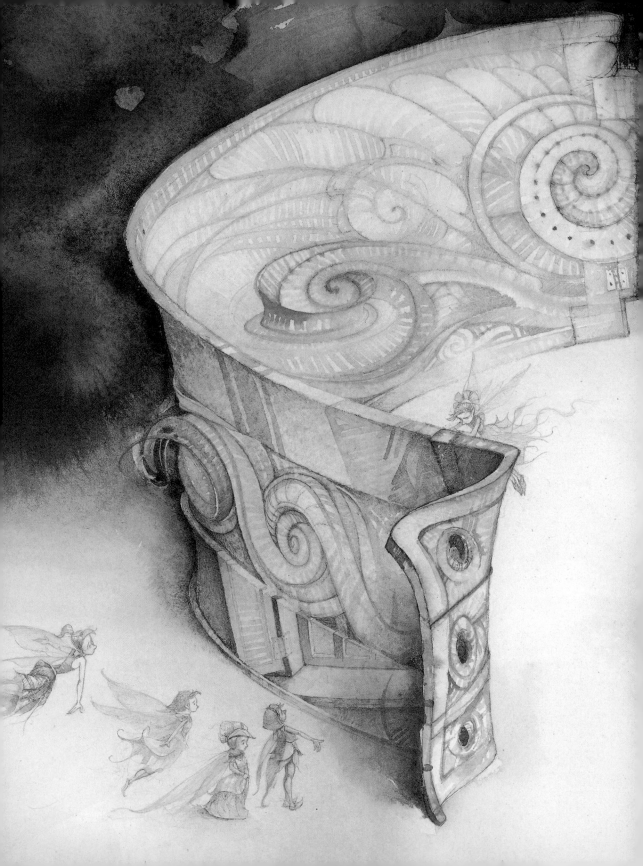

It was stunning, even though it was made of this and that, including the rims of sneaker lace holes. Copper nestled against silver against tin against gold. Gwendolyn thought she saw shapes—a goose, a fox, a bearded face. She looked away, looked back, and saw a rose, a sheep, a castle, her own house at Number 14.

The next morning Tink started work on the remaining parts of the Kyto Keeper: the three little screws for the collar, the big screw that would be sunk into the boulder, and, most demanding of all, the chain that would connect the collar to the big screw.

While Tink labored, sewing talents continued sewing the dragon suit together. Other preparations went forward as well in the next three days. The wing-washing talents scrubbed the wings of the fast fliers to give them maximum speed—once their wings dried. Fairies can't fly with wet wings. The water talents practiced making their water birds and flying them ever longer distances. And the cooking talents and baking talents wrapped food for the trip.

Gwendolyn was too big for most tasks, but she thought the singers might be able to use her. To prevent widespread fairy deafness, Queen Ree had banished the singers and the musicians to the fairy circle.

Gwendolyn waited until the orchestra took a break.

Crouching next to a singer, she asked if she could screech with them when she wasn't moving the boulder.

The singer, a fairy named Ellery, told Gwendolyn to open her mouth. Then she called over Juliette, another singer. Ellery rested her arms on Gwendolyn's lips and peered in. Over her shoulder she told Juliette, "Big space. Teeth are all right. Tongue is an excellent shape."

Gwendolyn felt proud of her tongue.

"Gums?" Juliette asked.

Ellery pulled Gwendolyn's lip down. "Healthy pink."

The two singers backed away. "Take a deep breath," Ellery said, "as deep as you can."

Gwendolyn inhaled so long she felt her toes expand. The

fairies nodded as the air streamed in, but when Gwendolyn couldn't pull in any more and began to exhale, they shook their heads.

"You'll be hoarse in ten minutes," Ellery said. "We can't have that."

"Oh." Gwendolyn felt ridiculous for being so disappointed. But she couldn't argue with talent.

"If someone wants a break," Ellery said kindly, "and we need a pinch screamer, you'll be first pick."

Gwendolyn nodded, feeling better.

Cymbals crashed, and the rehearsal was on again. Gwendolyn flew to her branch across from Mother Dove's nest. The uproar drowned out conversation. Mother Dove's neck pulsed, but Gwendolyn couldn't hear even a single coo.

After a few minutes the conductor stopped everyone to tell them how to worsen their performances. In the comparative silence, Mother Dove cooed, "Gwen-n-n-n-n-dol-l-l-l-l-yn-n-n-n-n-n," stretching the name out for so long that Gwendolyn became frightened.

"Is anything wrong, Mother Dove?"

"Gwen-n-n-n-n-dol-l-l-l-l-yn-n-n-n-n . . ."

Gwendolyn pressed her hands together so tight they hurt. "Tell me, Mother Dove."

"You try to be *beware*, but you don't always succeed."

Gwendolyn nodded miserably. "I know."

"You can stop seeing and hearing fairies even before you're grown up."

"What?" She was sure she hadn't heard right. "What?"

"If you harm a fairy, you could lose the ability to see and hear all fairies at that moment. If you harm a fairy tomorrow, you could lose the ability tomorrow."

Gwendolyn almost fell off her branch. She hiccupped and didn't think of the kiss. "Would you . . ." *Hic!* ". . . do that to me?" *Hic!*

"I wouldn't." Mother Dove cooed. "But Never Land might. It's just an island. It may not understand you mean well."

TWENTY-ONE

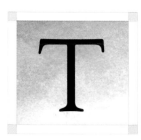

THAT NIGHT, Gwendolyn didn't have a kiss vision, although she stayed awake long enough to have a dozen. If she accidentally hurt a fairy before they reached Kyto, she wouldn't hear Tink tell her which boulder to move. She wouldn't know if her screeching was needed. She'd fail everyone.

In the morning she sought out Peter for information. She found him and the Lost Boys digging on the beach. Two

deep holes had already been dug, and water was seeping into both. The binoculars hung on a string around Peter's neck.

Only Peter and Curly had proper shovels. The others were using soup spoons, which they would probably eat from later without washing.

She hovered unseen. Was Peter angry at her because she'd failed to clean the entire underground home and hadn't darned a single sock?

He looked up and dropped his shovel. He stood, the image of astonishment. "Wendy! How did you get here?"

Gwendolyn landed, thinking, Can he have forgotten he brought me over?

"Gwendolyn," Tootles said.

"Oh, yes. It comes back to me. Would you like to dig for pirate treasure?" Gallantly, he offered his shovel.

Touched, she took it and began to dig.

Peter flew along the shore and returned with the biggest clamshell she had ever seen. He crouched nearby and dug too.

After a few minutes she asked, "Has Never Land ever gotten mad at you, Peter?"

"Nope." He dug deep and pulled out a huge load of sand, perfectly mounded, which he cast behind him.

Curly grinned, a sight seldom seen. "The island got rid of Skulk."

The Lost Boys lost their shyness in telling the tale. Skulk had been a Lost Boy, too, but not for long. He'd found a book of spells in a chest of pirate treasure and had cast one.

"The next time he flew," Tootles said, "the island slid away from under him."

"Did Never Land let him come back later?" Gwendolyn asked.

Curly smiled a second time, a record. "A shark probably ate him."

The island didn't seem very forgiving.

"Or . . ." Peter fairly spat the words: "The stupid boy grew up." Peter didn't forgive either.

Tootles said, "Skulk's spell made a grasshopper, and the island let it stay, the Never high hopper. It's everywhere now."

Gwendolyn changed the subject. "You've fought many battles, haven't you, Peter?"

Everyone laughed.

"Yes," Peter said.

"Suppose a . . . a monster attacked Never Land, what would you do?"

Peter put down his clamshell. "Big monster?"

"Very big."

"Scaly?"

"Scaly."

"Sharp teeth?"

"Very sharp."

"Flying?"

Gwendolyn didn't want him to guess Kyto. "Very fast runner, breathes out ice that freezes people in a second."

"I'd fight him."

Why did he think the monster was a him? "How?"

"With my sword. I'd kill him."

"Suppose you just wanted to capture it?"

"I'd dig a deep pit and chase him in and wouldn't let him climb out."

That wouldn't work with Kyto. "Who would you want helping you?"

Peter shrugged. "The Lost Boys could help if they wanted to."

A chorus rose. "We want to, Peter."

"Would you ask fairies to be on your side? Or would you think they were too little?"

"They're little, but they could help."

Tootles said, "Never underestimate a fairy."

I'm not, Gwendolyn thought, but they're so tiny, compared to a dragon. "How do you get ready for a fight with Captain Hook or wolves or a Never bear?"

Peter sat back on his haunches. "Buckle on my sword. Put my dagger in my belt."

"What do you *think* to get ready?"

"That I'm Peter." He hesitated. "That it has to be a fair fight."

Kyto wouldn't care about being fair.

"That we're gentlemen," Slightly said.

Gwendolyn nodded.

"That there's always another trick to try," Peter added.

Hmm, Gwendolyn thought.

"I think, Don't get cocky," Peter said. "And I never do."

The Twins coughed.

"Are you ever afraid?"

"Never."

Everyone dug in silence until Peter said, "That's enough. We'll try somewhere else."

Gwendolyn doubted their ideas would help, but she thanked them and excused herself.

At the Home Tree a multitude of fairies had gathered in the courtyard.

Tink and the other pots-and-pans talents had finished making the Kyto Keeper, and now they were polishing the chain, with fairy dust for polishing grit.

Marla, the cooking talent, asked why they were bothering. "Why does it have to look nice?"

Tink fixed Marla with her most scornful stare. "Beeecauzze," she said, dragging it out, "if the chain is beautiful and shiny and interesting, Kyto may not try to break it. Dragons love beauty. A magnificent chain may make him feel better about being captured."

The chain had twenty links, each link as long as Gwendolyn's hand, the metal twice as thick as her thumb.

Prilla turned a cartwheel above the chain, then leaned in close. "I'm twisty!" She laughed at her reflection. "My nose is above my eyes, and my mouth is sideways."

More fairies looked at themselves. Being *beware*, Gwendolyn waited until everyone had looked who wanted to. Then she flew to see, too.

Oof! Her face spread around a link. She had a doughnut face! She laughed. "Sprinkle on the sugar!"

Since everyone was assembled, Queen Ree announced which fairies were to go on the quest. She named ten dust talents, including Terence, ten scouts, ten nursing talents, five pots-and-pans talents plus Tink, and all the water talents and dairy talents and fast fliers and musicians and singers and light talents. Of the animal talents, only Beck was to come, and of the artists, only Bess, who had painted the face on the dragon suit. Three sewing-talent fairies were picked, to repair the suit if it tore. Dulcie and Marla were allowed to come, because they insisted they could make the food taste fresher.

Prilla, the only blinking talent, was included so she could start mainland Clumsy children clapping for fairies. Gwendolyn was coming to carry the boulder and for pinch-hit shrieking.

"We'll leave in the morning from the fairy circle," Queen Ree said. "Mother Dove will send us off."

The left-behind fairies had pale, depressed glows, but they got to work on the final defenses in case the expedition failed. They began by hiding Fairy Haven again, just as they had before Gwendolyn's arrival.

Gwendolyn said nothing, but what good would hiding do when Vidia, the traitor, knew exactly where everything was?

TWENTY-TWO

OG COVERED all of Fairy Haven. Gwendolyn's seventh day on the island began.

In the Home Tree courtyard, fairies were loading balloon-carrier baskets. Food went into one basket, the musicians' instruments into another. The basket for the Kyto Keeper was enormous, and its balloon was twice as big as the others, too big for Gwendolyn to hold in her arms.

After she lifted the Keeper inside, the dairy talents called her to hoist the dragon suit into its basket. The huge suit fit with room to spare because its cloth was as thin as a butterfly's wing.

Terence and another fairy-dust talent pulled the fairy-dust balloon carrier in from the mill.

Rani decided to ride with the Kyto Keeper. Tink put her in charge of the precious screws that would hold the collar closed.

Everyone was ready—or as ready as could be. Queen Ree carried Grandma's earring as a shield. Gwendolyn felt a thrill. The earring, going to battle!

The questers and the left-behinders followed Queen Ree to

Mother Dove's nest. When they arrived, Gwendolyn perched on her usual branch in the hemlock.

"Dears," Mother Dove cooed, "Kyto will be bigger than you expect, and his face will be purely evil. Don't give up hope. You have strengths he can't guess at."

Gwendolyn hoped for boulder-lifting strength she couldn't guess at and for a *beware* talent she hadn't shown so far.

"And now," Mother Dove said, "I offer this advice: Be nice to Vidia no matter what she does. Be nice even if she helps—"

"—Kyto," Rani finished. "Kyto?"

Mother Dove cooed. "Kyto."

Gwendolyn didn't want to be kind to Vidia. Still, obeying was sure to be part of being *beware*.

Queen Ree recited the traditional quest words, adjusting them to include Gwendolyn. "We'll be careful. We'll be kind. We'll be Never fairies and a Clumsy at our best. Follow me." She straightened her tiara and flew.

The other fairies streamed after her. The balloon carriers rose from the fairy circle as the sun pierced the fog. Gwendolyn shaded her eyes to watch, feeling herself a witness to history.

Once the balloon carriers cleared the forest canopy she began to fly, too. From above the hawthorn she looked down at Mother Dove, who had shrunk to the size of her hand. How does it feel to be her? Gwendolyn thought. She loves fairies as much as I do, but she can't go with them. As Gwendolyn soared away, she heard a plaintive note in Mother Dove's coos.

In five minutes she caught up with the questers. Her long shadow and the shadows of the balloon carriers glided across the treetops, but the fairies' shadows were too small to see.

Queen Ree said Gwendolyn bounced too much to pull a carrier. Instead, fast fliers towed the carriers in shifts.

Some fairies had never traveled this far from Fairy Haven. Gwendolyn oohed and aahed with them over the wonders below: a Never hairy lizard sunning on a rock, a grove of gigantic cypress trees, a field of scarlet daisies, a herd of long-nosed pigs.

When they weren't hauling balloon carriers, the fast fliers raced each other ahead and back. Sometimes Gwendolyn raced too, although she always lost. No matter how she tried she was no speedier than the average fairy.

"Hawk!" a scout shouted. "Hawk coming from the west!"

Fairies darted around in confusion. The sky offered no sanctuary.

Gwendolyn yelled, "Everyone! Behind me." A hawk against a Clumsy? Hah!

Fairies rushed to her until another scout cried, "Injured hawk. No danger."

Gwendolyn saw the hawk in the distance, a bird flying with a distinct limp.

Beck went to meet it while everyone else landed in a meadow and waited. After five minutes, she and the hawk descended. Its left wing was singed at the tip and still smoking.

The undersides of its wings were gold!

Prilla fluttered at Gwendolyn's ear. "He's the golden hawk."

Gwendolyn remembered the Golden Hawk constellation.

"There's only one like him." Prilla sounded awed. "He helped Rani change back to a fairy when she was a bat."

"Oh." Was that why Rani had Rani-bat in her head?

"His wing won't stop sizzling," Beck said. She soothed the hawk while a nursing talent spread ointment across his feathers and Terence sprinkled on fairy dust.

The smoke thinned and died out.

"How far away is Kyto?" Queen Ree asked.

"At the base of Torth," Beck said.

Tink said, "The hawk smoldered from there to here?"

"He tried to smother the embers on the ground," Beck said, "but they wouldn't go out."

Oh, no! Gwendolyn thought. Was dragon fire different from other fire?

"He thinks it might be the gold in his feathers or magic flames that kept him burning."

Rani burst out. "What if water makes his flames burn hotter? What if the water birds are useless?"

TWENTY THREE

ECK PATTED the hawk's wing, then stood. "He says Kyto is flying well, with a flat back, like our fast fliers. A fairy is with him."

Gwendolyn heard "sweet" and "darling" in angry voices as fairies railed against Vidia's treachery.

Now that he's flying strongly, she thought, he can attack before we reach the first boulder. If he did, the entire plan would fail.

The questers resumed flying. The golden hawk told Beck he'd stay with them as far as his nest.

They passed either north or south of the tiffens' banana farms, but not over them. Gwendolyn wondered whether the tiffens were preparing for Kyto or just debating, as Arli had predicted.

A scout called out the first sighting of the Wough, the widest river on the island.

Queen Ree exclaimed, "So soon! Excellent. The island is in a small mood."

Gwendolyn flew next to the Kyto Keeper carrier, where Terence and Tink were flying. "How can Never Land be in a small mood?"

Terence smiled. "Sometimes it is, and sometimes—"

"—it's in a large mood." Rani leaned over the edge of the basket.

Tink dimpled. "You never can tell."

The river came into view, and the golden hawk flew to his nest on its banks. Even by Clumsy standards, the Wough was mighty. A log raced downstream, borne on a powerful current.

Rani pulled out a leafkerchief and blew her nose. "The Wough is upset."

Terence said, "Because of—"

"—Kyto?" Rani nodded, wiping her eyes. "The river doesn't want its fish to boil."

Gwendolyn shuddered.

From across the swarm of fairies, Queen Ree announced there was no time to stop for lunch. Dulcie and Marla passed food around while they flew. Dulcie gave Gwendolyn a Clumsy-sized roll dotted with raisins and nuts. A quarter of the balloon-carrier basket for food was filled with rolls just like it, all of them for her.

Dulcie explained that the baking talents hadn't had time to make any other big food. "I'd fly backwards if I could."

"I've never tasted such delicious raisins," Gwendolyn said, meaning it. "Are the nuts pistachios?"

Dulcie nodded.

"I love pistachios."

"And the flour is our best rye, and the oil is pistachio, too." She smiled. "I'm so glad you like it."

The quest reached the plains at sunset. At first the fairies and Gwendolyn flew over a desert dotted with cactuses shaped like raindrops. Then, an hour later, in gathering darkness, boulders pricked up between the cactuses. Soon the boulders multiplied and the cactuses thinned, replaced by grass.

"Ree," Beck called, "I smell something." Although scouts had better eyesight and hearing than any other talent, animal talents had the best sense of smell.

Gwendolyn smelled only sweet grass.

Queen Ree went to Beck, who was flying next to the dragon-suit balloon carrier. Gwendolyn followed, along with Tink, Terence, and two scouts.

"Kyto?" Queen Ree asked.

Gwendolyn reached into her pocket for the kiss.

Beck closed her eyes. "Sweat, tooth decay, dirt, ash. It's Kyto."

A scout shouted, "Smoke ahead."

"Sh! Everybody whisper," Queen Ree whispered.

Scouts flew among the fairies, relaying the news.

"He's talking," a scout whispered.

To Vidia, of course.

"Can you hear any words?" Queen Ree asked.

"'Clover and' something 'roasted rabbit' something 'own recipe.' Oh! Vidia just said, 'You're my clever cooking' something 'darling.'"

Gwendolyn's stomach turned over. Roasted rabbit, roasted fairy. How could Vidia stay with him?

The scout's glow turned pale green. "Now I just hear chewing."

Queen Ree whispered, "Everyone, dim your glows."

Scouts scattered to give the order. The fairies dimmed their glows as much as they could. The light talents glowed no brighter than the Kyto Keeper.

Queen Ree whispered, "We'll land here."

The balloon carriers descended. Rani waved urgently from the Kyto Keeper basket. Gwendolyn saw and told Queen Ree.

"Don't land!" Rani shook her head, shedding tears. "We have to be near water."

Queen Ree had the quest head north, away from Kyto.

The stars hadn't risen, and the sky was almost black. Gwendolyn flew on her side to see behind her. Don't look our way, Kyto, she prayed. Don't hear us and don't smell us, not yet.

TWENTY FOUR

ANI YELLED, "Wa—" and whispered "—ter."

The questers landed on the south shore of a river that was narrower than the Wough but wide enough. Its current ran strong—it was uneasy, too. Rani splashed in while the other water talents waded up to their waists, their wings raised high. The fairies dipped their hands in and out and flicked their fingers. Each scoop of water became a water bird, darting and swooping above the river.

The musicians unloaded their instruments. Gwendolyn lifted the dragon suit out of its balloon carrier. Just as she finished spreading the suit on the grass, Queen Ree summoned everyone to the Kyto Keeper balloon carrier.

"Soon we will meet Kyto," she whispered. "Our goal is to divert his attention from the Kyto Keeper, which is more important than any one of us."

Fairies nodded. Gwendolyn shook her head. Saving even a single fairy life seemed more important than strategy.

As stars brightened the sky, dairy talents filed into the dragon suit. The cloth poked up here and there as they took their places. If the suit caught fire, they wouldn't be able to get out.

Are their wings feeling weak? Gwendolyn wondered. Are their hands icy? Are they wishing they hadn't volunteered?

The last dairy talent trooped in. A sewing talent stitched the opening closed. A scout squeezed into the slit at each of the dragon suit's eyes. The one at the right eye whispered, "Expand."

The suit swelled as the dairies pushed outward. The body rose on its legs, almost toppled, then straightened. Clinging to the snout were the light talents, who would be the flame, and the acting talents, who would be the voice. Fast fliers thrust their arms through straps on the underside of the wings.

Gwendolyn wondered if they wished for Vidia, the fastest of all.

The light talents raised and lowered their glows, unevenly, the way a fire burns. If they could only look hot, Gwendolyn thought. But they weren't fire talents. As far as she knew, there were no fire talents.

She went to Ree, who was with the right-eye scout. "There's no sizzle sound to the fire."

Queen Ree issued a command. A castanet player and a singer perched on the snout. The musician clicked the castanets and the singer hissed, between them imitating the snap and crackle of a real fire.

Flying backwards for a complete view, Gwendolyn saw that the suit, which was as big as an elephant, sagged.

Led by Terence, the fairy-dust talents scattered dust over the baggy suit. As the dust landed, the suit firmed. The light talents' glows heated up. Gwendolyn gasped, half afraid of being burned by this false, but oh-so-real, fire-belching dragon.

The suit rose, as smoothly as a real dragon. The dairy talents tucked in the legs neatly. As the suit started south, toward Kyto, its flame went out. A real dragon wouldn't flame without a reason.

Half the water talents, including Rani, herded water birds through the air. The rest remained at the river to create new birds and send them after the others.

Tink, Terence, and Prilla pulled the balloon carrier that held Rani and the Kyto Keeper. Gwendolyn started out with them, then flew away when a water bird hit her face and turned back into a drop of water.

The dragon suit's wing strokes created a back wind that slowed Gwendolyn and the other questers. The suit began to outstrip its followers.

Queen Ree shouted, "Wait!" She dropped her shield in the fairy-dust carrier basket so she could fly faster.

Other fairies shouted too, and Gwendolyn added her voice to the clamor, not caring if Kyto heard. If they weren't nearby when the suit met him, there would be no Kyto Keeper to capture him.

"Wait, suit, wait! Way-ay-ayt, soo-oo-oot!" Gwendolyn bellowed.

But the suit didn't hear. The wind must have been in the fast fliers' ears. Gwendolyn's wrists and ankles ached from pumping. Close by, fairies gasped for breath.

"Look!" a scout yelled.

Gwendolyn saw nothing except the dragon suit pulling away. Then, in the distance, a blot appeared against the starry sky. The blot grew and took shape. Huge wings. Long tail. Flat head. Smoke wreathing the snout.

Gwendolyn's heart clenched in fear.

The suit was close to Kyto now, but at least half a mile from the rest of the quest. The suit descended and landed amidst a field scattered with boulders. Kyto landed, too.

Did a tiny glow of light land with him? Was Vidia there?

The questers put every ounce of strength into their flying.

"Listen in!" Queen Ree panted to a scout, who already had a hand cupped around his ear.

"The suit is giving its greetings. Kyto is giving his greetings. He is asking how big the suit's hoard is and where it is."

Keep talking, suit and Kyto, Gwendolyn thought. Here we come! Nearly there!

"The suit is saying its home is across the sea and its hoard . . ." The scout trailed off as Kyto advanced on the suit, which flamed. Ignoring the light talents, he reached out a claw and jabbed the suit's belly.

The suit's skin took a moment to spring back.

Grinning, Kyto backed away and blew a ball of flame at the suit, which caught fire.

TWENTY·FIVE

A HUGE WIND whipped Gwendolyn around and blew her sideways. The dark earth rolled by beneath her. She screamed until her breath was gone. When the wind slammed her down, the ground was as soft as cookie dough. Clanks and rumbles rose from below. Boulders popped up and bounced.

Flailing his wings, failing to control his flight, his flame sputtering and snapping, Kyto swept by, going east. For an instant Gwendolyn felt his heat.

The earth tossed her into the air again. She was pulled, pushed, churned, spun by warring winds. Fairies and water birds eddied around her.

The fairies were laughing!

The dragon suit billowed and flapped in the midst of them, still burning. But the water birds, despite Rani's fear, were able to douse the fire.

Gradually the gale diminished to a breeze. The earth became solid again. Gwendolyn and the fairies, miraculously together, drifted to the ground. They were still on the plains. Boulders jutted here and there.

Gwendolyn sprawled on her back near a small tree with black bark. She groaned and sat up, brushing dirt and leaves from her face and school uniform. Above her, fairies still tumbled down, then righted themselves, and landed with grace and in Queen Ree's case, dignity.

The dragon suit, limp now, fell across two boulders. Its head, shoulders, and back were scorched. Gwendolyn could barely look at it, but she couldn't look away either. Were the dairy talents still inside, dead?

A leg jerked.

A sewing talent cut open a seam, and the dairy talents flitted out, uncrisped, even unsinged. They'd bunched together below the flames.

Gwendolyn's happiness lifted her back into the air, grinning down at the crowd of unharmed fairies below. Whatever had just happened, she thought, whatever had caused it—thanks! Thanks!

Three fairies tugged the food balloon carrier down close to a pile of white rocks. The other carriers made bumpy landings nearby. Queen Ree lifted her shield out of the dust carrier.

Gwendolyn flew to Prilla, who was loop-the-looping above the dragon suit. "Was that an earthquake?"

"No. Never Land stretched us away from Kyto. The island saved us." Prilla laughed. "Usually it doesn't stretch so fast."

The power of Never Land! Gwendolyn thought.

Queen Ree flew to a light talent who had perched in the tree. Gwendolyn followed.

"Was Vidia with Kyto?" Queen Ree asked.

Fairies hung in the air to hear the answer. Gwendolyn held her breath.

"She was there, above his head. When he flamed, she flew away."

"She didn't help him?" Queen Ree said.

The light talent answered, "No. She didn't."

Silence lingered a moment, then laughter and chatter resumed.

She didn't stop him! Gwendolyn thought indignantly.

Tink asked Gwendolyn and Terence to help land the Kyto Keeper carrier. When it was down, Rani climbed out.

"Is Kyto gone for good?" Gwendolyn asked as she weighted the carrier basket with stones.

Tink tugged her bangs. "He'll be back."

The stars dimmed and the sun rose on Gwendolyn's eighth day.

Queen Ree decided the questers should remain where they were. "We'll let Kyto come to us. He'll look now. He must be very angry."

She flew above everyone and called down, "These are our boundaries." She flew to the tree. "This tree." She flew on. "This rock pile. This petrified log."

They formed a triangle, each marker roughly a city block apart, a large area for fairies, not so big for a dragon.

Rani guided the water birds to earth, where they dissolved, making mud. With a gathering gesture, she drew the mud together into a fairy-sized pond, a puddle to Gwendolyn. Water birds dived down in a narrow waterfall, sent by the water talents who'd stayed behind at the river.

Rani laughed. "We'll drown him."

Drown one of his claws, Gwendolyn thought, not joining in the laughter.

Dulcie and Marla distributed food. Gwendolyn bit into another raisin-nut roll, which still tasted fresh.

Tink flew to her. "I have to find the right boulder. Come."

Terence came too, of course. Tink flew from boulder to boulder until she arrived at a squarish one near the pile of white rocks. She flew around it, then walked around it. She felt it here and sniffed it there. "Do you like dragons or not like them?"

Terence lighted atop the boulder. He told Gwendolyn, "She's speaking to the metal in the rock."

"Will you help Kyto or fairies?" Tink leaned her ear against it to listen.

The boulder stood almost as tall as Gwendolyn. She was certain she couldn't lift it, unless . . . "Terence, would I be stronger if I ate fairy dust?"

He laughed so hard he cried.

Gwendolyn smiled uncomfortably.

When Terence caught his breath he said, "No." He giggled. "Every fairy-dust talent tries it sometime or other." Another explosion of mirth. "It tickles on your insides! For days!"

"I see." Gwendolyn touched the boulder, which felt cold and unfriendly. If it could talk, it would probably tell her how puny she was.

"It won't help Kyto," Tink announced. "It may help us."

"How deep into the ground does the boulder go?" Gwendolyn asked.

"Two inches," Tink said promptly.

Only two inches. Not bad, Gwendolyn thought, and if it hates dragons, maybe it will lift itself. Or maybe Never Land would heave it up. Gwendolyn crouched and felt around the base, searching for spots for her hands when the time came. A gopher hole curved under the rock. She eased her hand in and hoped not to be bitten.

"Don't prod me, love."

"What?" Gwendolyn jerked her hand out.

A fairy's head and shoulders emerged from the opening. The fairy flew out, stretched, and yawned. "Dear hearts, what are you doing here?"

Vidia!

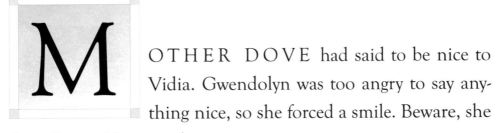

TWENTY-SIX

OTHER DOVE had said to be nice to Vidia. Gwendolyn was too angry to say anything nice, so she forced a smile. Beware, she thought, and kept smiling.

Terence nodded at Vidia.

Tink, whose idea of *nice* was different from anyone else's, said, "Go away."

"Fly with you too, darling."

Queen Ree landed at Vidia's side. "Fly with you."

"Where's Kyto, Ree, dear?"

"Gone," Tink said.

"Sweets, is he coming back?"

Terence said, "We think so."

"I need everyone's help." Queen Ree adjusted her tiara. "Yours too, Vidia."

"No. Not mine, dear hearts. I don't want any part of it." She streaked away.

Vidia is frightened, Gwendolyn thought.

Queen Ree called, "We miss you, Vidia."

"Too nice," Terence muttered.

Divided loyalty. . . . Nothing divided by nothing. Vidia was worthless.

"This is the boulder," Tink told Queen Ree.

Gwendolyn flew the Kyto Keeper from its balloon-carrier basket. She hovered, holding it. "If I put it down, it will get dirty."

The dairy talents spread the dragon suit across the boulder, and Gwendolyn set the Keeper on top, in the middle of the cloth that hadn't burned. The sewing talents cut away the blackened sections.

Queen Ree had everyone else move nearby so they'd be ready when Kyto returned.

But the water-bird puddle was far away, by the tree.

Rani cried, "Water talents, go!"

The other water talents spaced themselves evenly around the puddle. They squatted and lifted it, exactly the way Clumsies might lift a picnic blanket. The puddle sagged, but no water spilled.

Gwendolyn wished she could photograph it. Instead, she memorized the jiggle of the surface water, the droop at the bottom, and the surprised frog hopping in the puddle's shadow.

The water talents put the puddle down a few yards from the boulder. Rani waved in newly arriving water birds. More dived in every moment.

Queen Ree ordered the fairy-dust balloon carrier to be tethered to the petrified log, as far as possible from the Kyto Keeper. "We don't want Kyto near our fairy dust. Park all the carriers there, so they don't catch fire."

Or are less likely to catch fire, Gwendolyn thought. For who knew what Kyto's tactics would be?

The sewing talents took out their scissors and snipped the grass down to the ground to keep any fire from spreading. Other fairies pulled grass by hand.

Gwendolyn pulled out fistfuls. A sewing talent grinned up at her.

When the grass was cleared, Queen Ree declared a rest. "We'll need our strength soon enough." She stretched out on the dragon suit, placing her shield so it shaded her head.

A scout lay on either side of her. Tink settled next to the Keeper collar, with her polishing cloth for a pillow. Terence sat back against the collar, his lap an inch from Tink's head. Below, Beck curled around an anthill.

Gwendolyn flew to where the grass began again and lay down. She missed her bower. The sky seemed too bright for sleep, but she closed her eyes and thought about the power of Never Land—to glide across the ocean, to stretch or shrink, to let a girl see and hear fairies forever or deprive her forever.

She felt in her skirt pocket to see if the kiss felt warm. It did, but there was no vision, only the sound of crackling. Wherever he was, Kyto was flaming.

Kyto, use up your flame, she thought as she slipped into nightmares of fires and boiling prairie rivers.

Dulcie woke her by putting a raisin-nut roll into her open hand. The sun was high in the sky. The puddle had grown into a Clumsy-sized pond.

Tink was twisting the Kyto Keeper chain's big screw into the side of the boulder below the dragon suit. The screw wound in as easily as if the boulder were butter. The metal in the rock, Gwendolyn thought, loves the metal screw.

There. Tink finished. The boulder choice was permanent.

Please, Gwendolyn thought, let Kyto land close enough that I don't have to lift it.

Around her, several fairies still slept. Beck snored into her anthill. Tink returned to polishing the chain.

Terence flew over the Kyto Keeper, then landed by Tink. He coughed in an embarrassed way. "Erm . . . Tink, do you want Kyto to see the Keeper?"

Head down, still polishing, Tink said, "I have to—" She looked up. "He mustn't see it!"

Tink and Terence coiled the Keeper chain and the collar atop the boulder. Gwendolyn draped the suit over it, leaving a corner of boulder showing. The art talent Bess improved on her draping, so the suit seemed to have been dropped carelessly on an ordinary boulder.

Beck jumped up from the anthill. "Something is wrong." Her voice rose. "*Nooo!*"

A scout yelled, "Kyto!"

Gwendolyn's knees went weak.

Beck whispered, "He has Mother Dove."

TWENTY-SEVEN

Q UEEN REE flew to Beck. "Has he hurt Mother Dove?"

Beck just rocked.

"Has he hurt her?" Queen Ree shook Beck's shoulder so hard her own tiara fell off. "Is she still on the egg?"

A scout shouted, "He has the nest and Mother Dove!"

As delicately as she could, Gwendolyn put Queen Ree's tiara back on.

Except for Tink, who air-paced above the boulder, her hand on her dagger, and Beck, who was still rocking, everyone else hung still and drooped, even Queen Ree.

Gwendolyn thought there might be reason for hope. "How do we know *he* has *her*? She's the wisest creature. He's carrying her, but *she* might really have *him*."

Queen Ree's shoulders straightened. "She might."

A surge of energy ran through the fairies. Musicians took up their instruments and began to untune them. Singers sang off-key scales. Scouts formed a line on either side of Queen Ree.

Beck continued to rock.

Terence, Prilla, and Tink rushed to the balloon carriers and back to the Kyto Keeper, carrying the three collar screws. Four more dust talents came with them, bearing dust sacks.

Tink tucked the screws under the dragon suit. A dust talent wormed himself all the way under, where Gwendolyn was sure he slathered fairy dust on the Kyto Keeper and the boulder. The other three spilled dust, much more than a day's allotment, on Gwendolyn and the fairies who were going to help with the lifting. Gwendolyn's tingle was so sharp it hurt.

The dot in the sky swelled into Kyto. A moment later he was directly above, throwing Gwendolyn and the fairies into shadow. He dropped quickly and landed on the other side of the pond, about fifteen yards from the boulder, between the pile of rocks and the petrified log.

Hate poured out of him, out of his orange eyes and smoking nostrils and red mouth, even out of his scales and the barbs on his spine.

Gwendolyn gripped the boulder to hold herself up. His hate and his stench seeped into her, leaching away hope.

How could they defeat him? He was too big, too powerful,

too cruel, for fairies and a Clumsy to overcome.

Mother Dove didn't even fill his front claws. Her serenity shone through his hatred, such serenity that she might have been at home in her hawthorn. If Mother Dove isn't afraid, Gwendolyn thought, fighting despair, she must think it will be all right.

Or she was acting brave for her fairies.

"Fairies . . ." Kyto smiled, showing a thousand yellowed stiletto teeth.

Mother Dove said, "He stuffed his ears with mud when I tried to coo him to sleep. He can't hear anything. Everyone at Fairy Haven is well."

If he couldn't hear, the musicians and singers wouldn't be able to distract him.

"I'll make him sleep," Beck said. She tilted her head, sank to her knees, then toppled.

Gwendolyn gasped. Had Beck died?

Kyto's eyes closed, opened, seemed out of focus.

He was growing sleepy! Beck was alive, her mind burrowing into Kyto's.

But his eyes regained focus and stayed open.

Prilla said, "I'll blink for sleep."

Gwendolyn thought, She's blinking to make Clumsy children clap. I can clap. He can't hear me, so I can clap. She clapped as hard as she could, rat-a-tatting across the prairie. Clapping made her feel better. She was doing something.

His head swayed . . . straightened . . . swayed . . . and straightened.

Flames curled around his lips. Water talents made a column of water birds rise from the pond and hover, ready. But Kyto's eyes closed and stayed shut. The flames died away to smoke. His head slumped to the ground.

"Lift!" Tink said in Gwendolyn's ear.

She stopped clapping.

Kyto's neck stretched away from the boulder, increasing the distance the boulder had to travel, but enabling an approach from behind. Gwendolyn's hands found grips at the base. Dulcie and Marla perched atop the dragon suit to prevent it from slipping off. Along with Tink and the other pots-and-pans talents and Terence and the other dust talents and the dairy talents and the fast fliers and the sewing talents and the light talents and the nursing talents and Bess, Gwendolyn lifted.

Strain ran through her arms into her torso, her legs, her feet. Her fingers were in agony, and the hopeless feeling engulfed her again. Still, she straightened, her eyes on Kyto. With the fairies she carried the boulder and the Keeper, one step, two steps, three. They had about sixty more steps to his head.

How could they lug this weight another sixty steps?

He lay on his side, his claws stretched in front of him, with Mother Dove still cupped in them. Smoke drifted from his nostrils and between his lips.

Mother Dove could have flown away if it weren't for her egg. Scouts drew near to lift out the nest, but they hesitated, clearly afraid of waking him.

"Don't let the suit slip!" Tink yelled. Despite Dulcie and Marla's efforts, the dragon suit was sliding away.

Fairies flew to fix the suit. Without their strength Gwendolyn almost dropped the boulder.

Four steps. Five steps. The fairies helped again.

Ten steps. Twelve. Twenty. They were behind the tip of his tail. Thirty steps. Halfway there!

Gwendolyn's hands were slick with sweat. She didn't know how she was going to keep her grip.

Kyto's eyelids fluttered.

"Set it down," Tink called.

They eased the boulder to the ground. While gasping for breath, Gwendolyn resumed clapping.

With the scary grace of a snake, Kyto's head and neck undulated upward. Peeping out from behind the boulder, Gwendolyn saw him in profile. His eye blinked twice, then stayed open. He belched a puff of flame, which arced downward into the dirt and sputtered out. Grunting, he lifted himself onto his back legs.

Beck still lay where she'd fallen.

Kyto, Gwendolyn thought, please don't notice that the dragon suit has moved. Luckily, he didn't turn his head.

Carrying her shield, Queen Ree flew to him and landed in the shadow of his snout. She can do nothing, Gwendolyn thought.

He raised Mother Dove as high as his mouth, her feathers glowing yellow in his breath.

Queen Ree lowered the shield, took off her tiara, and placed both on the ground in front of her. The message was clear. Let go of Mother Dove and you can have the Never fairy queen's tiara and shield for your hoard.

Kyto balanced himself on one back claw. Gwendolyn kept clapping. His eyes closed, then opened. He extended his free back claw, threaded a claw tip into Queen Ree's tiara, wrapped another talon around the shield, and pulled them in.

"Queen Clarion, now I have your crown, your shield, and your Mother Dove." He smirked. "Since fire won't hurt her, I will eat her without flaming. I like my food raw sometimes."

"My egg!" Mother Dove cried.

Kyto opened his cavernous mouth.

"Help!" Gwendolyn shouted, still clapping. "Never Land!"

TWENTY-EIGHT

OVE!" A sparkle darted in from beyond the balloon carriers, grew into Vidia, and landed next to Queen Ree.

Mother Dove cooed, "Vid-d-d-ia . . . Vid-d-d-ia . . ."

Kyto moved Mother Dove away from his mouth and smiled. "Vidia! My fast flameling!" He tilted Mother Dove and her nest into his right claw.

The egg teetered on the claw's edge and tipped.

With a wing, Mother Dove swept it to safety under her.

Using his left claw, Kyto pulled the mud out of his ears.

Gwendolyn stopped clapping.

Vidia perched on Mother Dove's back, inches from Kyto's snout. "Kyto, sweet, I need her feathers. She has to live to make them."

Brave, Vidia! Gwendolyn thought. She loves Mother Dove too much to let her die.

Kyto considered. "Can't you—"

"Darling, without fairy dust I can barely fly."

Kyto yawned.

Gwendolyn clapped softly, one hand just patting the other until Tink's *"Sh!"* exploded in her ear.

Kyto's shoulders swiveled away from the Kyto Keeper.

"Move!" Tink whispered.

They carried the boulder and the Kyto Keeper five more steps while Kyto set Mother Dove near the musicians and singers, who were silent but poised to play.

Mother Dove was safe! Now her wisdom could help. And Vidia could help.

As Kyto straightened, his back to Gwendolyn and the others, they kept going, noiselessly. A few more minutes and they'd reach him.

He flew to a spot halfway between the musicians and the tree. Gwendolyn and the others put the boulder down. He was facing it now, and he was far too far away. She held the kiss and bit back a groan.

"Come to me, glowing opal!" he called.

Vidia flew to his shoulder. "Darling, you are flying beautifully."

He craned his neck to look at her. "Thank you."

"Move it!" Tink whispered.

They carried the Kyto Keeper four steps, then four more while Kyto's head was turned. Useless, Gwendolyn thought. The distance was three times what it had been when they'd started.

"Kyto . . ." Queen Ree began, flying to him again. She reached up to adjust her tiara, but there was no tiara. She lowered her hand. "We mean you no harm. We—"

He laughed, really laughed.

Gwendolyn exhaled in relief. Nothing terrible would happen if he was happy and wasn't feeling all that hatred.

Vidia flew off his shoulder and perched on a boulder a few yards from him. "I can watch better from here, my love."

She's afraid, Gwendolyn thought, noticing the flicker in her glow. Why, if he's happy?

"Don't look away, brightness."

The musicians and singers started their racket. He turned to them, startled.

"Lift!" Tink whispered.

Gwendolyn felt for her handholds while still peeking out.

A flutist flew toward Mother Dove.

Kyto spat a blob of flame and hit the flutist. The water birds put out some of it. Gwendolyn forgot to lift or obey or *beware*.

The flutist's wings ignited, then the rest of her. Fairies shouted. Mother Dove cawed.

Beside herself, Gwendolyn popped out from behind the boulder, jumping up and down in distress, tears streaming. Kyto could have seen her if he'd looked, or maybe he did look and judged her unimportant.

Her thoughts came in short bursts. The Kyto Keeper would never reach Kyto. They'd never trap him. He'd kill the fairies here. He'd fly to Fairy Haven and kill the fairies there. Never fairies gone forever. Extinct, except for Vidia.

Kyto belched fire toward the musicians and singers. The water birds put out the flame, but Gwendolyn, blinded by tears, didn't see.

She had to save fairies! Had to, had to, had to! She could think of only one way. Take them to the house at Number 14.

She pulled off her backpack, shrieking, "Fairies! Come to me!" Her shouts may have been the reason a fireball flared over the Kyto Keeper.

Through her tears she saw a spark catch Tink's scalloped skirt. Tink fell and rolled on the ground, aflame. Not Tink! Gwendolyn leaped, hand outstretched, and grabbed her. She smothered the flame in her hand, not even feeling the heat.

"You're safe," she whispered, holding tight.

Tink kicked and fought, but Gwendolyn wouldn't let go. "I'm saving you."

Tink went slack. Good, Gwendolyn thought. She understands.

She unzipped her backpack, thrust Tink inside, and zipped it up. Now to rescue more fairies.

She felt a jolt from the earth, from Never Land, slamming through the bones in her feet and up from joint to joint. Her chin hit her chest.

Was the island saving fairies again?

Through the smoke Kyto was still flaming. Never Land hadn't helped. It was up to her. She had to catch more fairies.

But she didn't see Rani or the other water talents around the pond. Had Kyto gotten them?

She didn't hear any fairy shouts, but Mother Dove was calling Tink.

"I have her!" Gwendolyn yelled. She saw no fairies around the dragon suit. No flying scouts. No dust talents at the balloon carrier. Were they embers too?

"Tin-n-n-k," Mother Dove cooed, then, "Gwen-n-n-dol-l-l-yn-n-n. Gwen-n-n-dol-l-l-yn-n-n."

No Vidia on her boulder. Where was she? He wouldn't have crisped her. She had to be there. But she wasn't.

Then Gwendolyn understood. She couldn't see or hear fairies.

EVER LAND is wrong! Gwendolyn thought. I'm not hurting Tink, I'm saving her, and I'll save more.

Grown-ups could feel fairies, even if they couldn't see them. Hiccuping and weeping, she groped along the dragon suit. Aha! A squirming, twisting fairy! Gwendolyn shoved her or him in her backpack and zipped it.

She caught four more fairies, then couldn't find any others. They must have been flying from her, their rescuer.

"Come to me," she cried, holding out her hands. "I'll take you to safety."

No fairies came. Kyto huffed a fireball straight at her, but the water birds doused it.

She gave up. Six fairies would live. She hugged the backpack against her chest to keep them from worming out. As she flew over the fairy-dust balloon carrier basket, she reached in for enough fairy dust sacks to get her home. She stuffed them in her skirt pocket on top of the kiss.

Then she headed east. Every few minutes she glanced back, expecting to see Kyto in pursuit. After a while, the smoke along the horizon faded into clear blue.

Through the waning afternoon, Gwendolyn flew over the plains. At sunset, a herd of curly-maned horses galloped by below. She wondered if Kyto would crisp them after finishing off fairies.

A few trees loomed ahead in the dark, then more and more. She had come to the forest that the Wough River ran through. Without realizing, she flew lower. She could reach down and touch the uppermost leaves. It wasn't a lack of fairy dust. It was exhaustion.

She landed in a pine grove carpeted with pine needles, just like the bed in her bower. She lay on her side with her arms through the backpack straps. Something tapped her forearm. No use kicking, she thought and closed her eyes.

Her dreams were of fairies. Rani taught her how to make water birds. Prilla blinked in and away, begging Gwendolyn to clap for fairies. Vidia landed on Gwendolyn's hand repeatedly, crying, "Throw me!"

The last dream was of Tink, zipping back and forth in front of her face. First she tugged her bangs and said, "Lift! Carry the boulder." Then she dimpled and said, "It's called a bower," while Mother Dove squawked, "You weren't *beware*. You harmed fairies."

When Gwendolyn woke, the backpack lay near her head. She pulled it closer and spotted a hole in the bottom, big enough for a fairy to squirm through.

Tink's dagger!

Frantically, Gwendolyn felt around the ground. Nothing. She waved her hands in the air. Nothing.

She had failed to save a single fairy.

The hiccups came in waves. She didn't bother to reach for the kiss. She deserved to hiccup forever.

If she went back for more fairies, they'd all fly from her, if any were still alive.

Sitting up, she emptied a sack of fairy dust over her head. She would go to Peter, who had fought so many fights and could see fairies.

Sorry, Mother Dove, she thought. You didn't want Peter in this battle.

But probably Peter would be too late. How could any fairies have survived the night?

She began flying anyway. Tootles had said not to underestimate fairies. Maybe some were still alive. The Wough River roiled beneath her and caught a few of her tears. Peter had said always to have another trick to try. She hadn't had a first trick.

If only Kyto had been a puzzle! Then she might have solved him. But how? What could have defeated him?

Dulcie could have baked a cake that would have put him to sleep.

Could Gwendolyn go to Fairy Haven now and have them make one?

They had no cake pans.

If the questers had had something to bargain with they might have controlled him. But he had his freedom and could take whatever he wanted.

Had Mother Dove given any clues? She'd said, *Be kind to Vidia*, and Vidia had saved Mother Dove. Good advice for herself but not for fairies.

Gwendolyn's flight slowed.

Be kind to Vidia. Mother Dove loved her fairies. She wouldn't have been thinking of herself.

Be kind to Vidia.

Because Vidia was needed and, of course, Mother Dove loved her.

Ah, yes. Vidia was the key.

Gwendolyn turned and dumped another sack of fairy dust on her head for speed. She was going back. If any fairies were still alive, Vidia could save the rest.

Gwendolyn thought, But first Never Land will have to help me.

✳

Returning felt faster than leaving. The island must have shrunk again.

As she flew she was tormented by the memory of Tink going slack in her hand.

By noon she saw a smudge ahead, which could have been merely a lingering haze. If Kyto and Mother Dove were gone and the Kyto Keeper was still there, she'd know that fairies had lost.

When she reached the first landmarks, the balloon carriers and the petrified log, she began to cough. The smoke was so thick she could barely make Kyto out.

But there he was, still flaming, and water birds were still dousing most of his flame, so at least one water talent was alive. Hope gave Gwendolyn a burst of speed, as if she'd flashed through a shower of fairy dust.

The pond was a puddle again, a small puddle.

Kyto trumpeted, "Little crispiness, see? I got another one!"

Another one! Gwendolyn peered into the smoke. There! Mother Dove sat on her nest on the ground, her feathers gray with soot, her serenity gone. She was sobbing!

The dragon suit over the Kyto Keeper was where it had been before, still an impossible distance from Kyto's neck.

Now, Never Land! Gwendolyn thought. Know what

I need. Show me one fairy, just Vidia. Show me Vidia.

Gwendolyn squinted into the murk. There was the tall boulder Vidia had perched on, but she wasn't visible there or on Kyto's head and shoulders.

"Glitter light, are you watching?"

"I'm watching, love."

Gwendolyn heard her!

"Observe, speedy glowworm." Kyto's gaze shifted.

Gwendolyn followed his eyes and saw her! Vidia! Glowing an excited orange, she buzzed back and forth between the puddle and the petrified log, always facing Kyto, watching fairies Gwendolyn couldn't see.

Thank you, Never Land!

Flying low, Gwendolyn approached from the puddle, sneaking in behind Vidia. She drew closer, closer, closer. She reached, grabbed—got her!

Kyto shouted, "Sizzle! Roast! Fry! Crisped another fairy!"

Vidia wriggled and kicked in Gwendolyn's right hand. With her left, Gwendolyn pressed Vidia's wings together and reminded herself that wings didn't feel pain. She landed a dragon length from the Kyto Keeper boulder and yelled, "Kyto! I have Vidia!"

His head swung around. "Is that the human child? Has she returned?"

The smoke must have been hard for him to see through, too. "Yes. I have Vidia."

Vidia squeaked, "Ouch! Ouch, darling. She's hurting me!"

Gwendolyn knew she wasn't. Vidia was pretending—helping!

Kyto landed close to the Kyto Keeper, with his back to it, his furious face turned toward Gwendolyn.

Tink, I need you, Gwendolyn thought. Don't let me have killed you. She shouted, "I'll squeeze Vidia to death unless you stop roasting fairies."

Behind him, the dragon suit slid away to reveal the Kyto Keeper.

Kyto held out a claw for Vidia. "I won't hurt another fairy."

The collar rose a few inches. The three collar screws rose too.

"I don't believe you!" Gwendolyn yelled.

"Love, she's got my wings!"

Thank you, Vidia!

Kyto's eyes darkened from orange to purple.

The collar and chain inched through the air above his tail.

"Prove you'll stop crisping fairies!" Gwendolyn had no idea how he could prove it.

"I swear I'll stop." Flames licked his lips.

The collar opened wide at its hinge.

"Prove it!" *Hic!*

"Ouch! Sweet, hurry!"

He blew smoke at Gwendolyn's feet. Oh! So hot! Ouch! Oh! But she couldn't fly away or he'd come after her and leave the Kyto Keeper behind.

The collar was above his back, heading for his neck.

"I won't let her go until you prove it!" Gwendolyn cried.

Sss! A tongue of flame licked Gwendolyn's skirt. He was going to kill them both! Looking down, terrified, not thinking, she loosened her hold on Vidia—

—who didn't fly away, didn't budge. "The Clumsy is crushing me!"

Gwendolyn's hem sizzled. She held Vidia tight again and leaned sideways, trying to keep the skirt from touching her legs. "Prove it!"

The collar was almost at his neck. Her hem erupted into flame. "Only a moment more," she whispered to Vidia.

The collar closed around his neck. The screws were going in.

"Only a moment more," she repeated. Then she would let go and roll on the ground and put herself out. "Only a moment more."

He blew a fireball at her.

The water birds doused most of it, and the rest blew past her head, but her skirt was blazing. Still gripping Vidia, she rolled on the ground.

Had they closed the collar?

She rolled and rolled.

Was Never Land safe?

The pain!

A bird's wings beat at her skirt.

Her mind flickered and went out.

**G**WENDOLYN woke to aching and smarting thighs. She opened her eyes, which crossed instantly. Two Tinks were perched on her nose, both dimpling.

But I can't see fairies, she thought, ignoring her pain. Could it be? Tink? In plain view, visible again?

She closed her eyes, then popped them open. The double Tink was still there. "I'm dreaming." Even so, and despite her legs, she smiled her wide first-fairy-sighting smile.

Tink flew away, shouting, "Gwendolyn's awake!"

I heard that! Gwendolyn thought. She raised her head.

Before she could view her surroundings, a different fairy—
not Tink—pushed her forehead back down. Another fairy
leaned on her chin. A third whispered in her ear. "Rest. Sleep."

Her head settled onto something soft. She closed her eyes,
but sleep was impossible. Fairies audible and visible again. Tink
again. Terence, Queen Ree, Prilla, Rani, Dulcie, all of them—if
they were all alive.

Kyto!

She jumped up, although her head swam and her legs hurt
worse than before. She swayed, then found her balance.

There Kyto was, asleep, chained to the boulder with the
Kyto Keeper collar around his neck. Vidia perched on his
shoulder.

Nursing talents circled Gwendolyn and insisted she sit.
When she was seated, they lifted her skirt up to her thighs,
which shone as red as an apple.

"Your old skirt burned," a fairy said, spreading salve, quarter inch by quarter inch. The dabs of salve soothed the pain
down to a dull ache.

The new skirt was covered with dragon scales. Gwendolyn
touched a scale, which felt bumpy with paint. Nursing talents
drew the dragon-suit skirt back down. Naturally it fit perfectly.
Sewing talents, of course.

Gwendolyn was nested in the rest of the dragon suit, in the cloth that hadn't been needed for her skirt. Her backpack, with Tink's dagger's hole neatly darned, lay at the edge of the suit.

Tink returned with Queen Ree, Terence, and Prilla. They were alive!

"Tink?" Gwendolyn said. "Did I hurt you?"

She tugged her bangs. "No."

But Terence sounded reproachful. "You knocked the wind out of her."

"I'd fly backwards if I could."

"Never mind," Tink said, scowling at Terence.

"Your tiara, Queen Ree?" Gwendolyn said. "He still has it?"

"And your gift. I'd fly backwards if I could." Her glow reddened. Queen Ree rarely apologized.

"It's all right, but your tiara is more—"

"He can keep it. A souvenir of being captured by fairies."

"And a Clumsy," Tink said, smiling again.

Gwendolyn blushed. "The last thing I remember is catching fire. What happened next?"

Prilla said, "Kyto was so angry at you and so worried about Vidia that he didn't feel the collar until the screws were in."

Queen Ree laughed. "You found the perfect method of distracting him!"

Prilla added, "Then we all got out of the way of his flame."

"How did I get out of the way?"

"You rolled," Terence said.

"Wings flapped on me."

A crowd gathered. Rani, dripping wet, walked toward Gwendolyn. The water-bird puddle had swollen into a pond again.

"Were there really wings?" Gwendolyn asked. "Did the golden hawk come—"

"—back? No." Rani's voice became reverent and teary. "Mother Dove left the nest to put out your fire."

"She did? For me?" Mother Dove never left the nest. Gwendolyn rose onto her knees to look for her. "Is the egg all right?"

"She left it for only a minute," Queen Ree said.

Tink added, "The air was so hot, the egg was safe."

"Lie down," a nursing talent said.

Ah, Gwendolyn thought. There was the nest, still near the musical instruments, and there was Mother Dove, serene again. Beck was with her, feeding her something.

"Beck's alive!"

"Lie down," the nursing talent repeated more forcefully.

Gwendolyn settled herself on the dragon suit. She still had a dozen questions, especially the one she was afraid to ask, so she asked a different one instead. "When did I let go of Vidia?"

Laughing, Prilla did a handstand on Gwendolyn's chest. "You didn't. She squirmed free."

Gwendolyn leaned up on one elbow. "Did I hurt—"

"—her? She didn't say."

"Erm . . ." Queen Ree cleared her throat. "Did Vidia really help you?"

Gwendolyn nodded. "Otherwise I would have failed. I let go of her by accident, but she stayed. Even though I wasn't hurting her, she said I was."

"The fast fliers are not disgraced." Queen Ree reached up for the missing tiara. "She saved us, but she's with him now."

Vidia was complicated, two fairies in one, a loyal traitor.

Gwendolyn's eyes closed. She mumbled, "What about . . ."

As she faded she heard a nursing talent say, "She's still weak, but she's out of danger."

What danger? She was asleep before she could ask.

When Gwendolyn woke up again, her legs no longer hurt. Prilla and Rani were dozing on her blouse. Taking care not to wake them, she felt around until she found the pocket in her new skirt. No kiss.

THIRTY-ONE

THE SILVER around the kiss must have melted, and the acorn button had probably burnt up. It was a terrible loss, history destroyed. Mother and Grandma would take it hard. Gwendolyn wondered how her neck would get used to being permanently without the chain.

And the visions were gone too. Oh, how she'd miss her glimpses of Never Land! There would be no news unless Peter remembered to come.

But she'd have memories and her imagination. It would be easy now to picture the Home Tree and invent new adventures.

Prilla poked Rani's shoulder. "Gwendolyn's eyes are open."

Rani walked from Gwendolyn's blouse to her skirt. Gwendolyn sat up.

Kyto stood by the boulder, awake too and holding the Kyto Keeper chain up to his face. Gwendolyn wondered if he was admiring himself or trying to snap a link.

Vidia fluttered around his head. Tink stood on the ground

on the other side of the boulder, out of the way of his flame, stroking the rock and talking. Terence hovered nearby, closer than Tink usually allowed him.

"Is Terence helping Tink?" Gwendolyn asked.

Prilla did a somersault on Gwendolyn's skirt. "I doubt it. She admitted she missed him when she was in your backpack."

Good for Terence at last, Gwendolyn thought. "I see fewer fairies than when I woke up before." Nervously, she bunched a handful of skirt in her hands. "Did anything—"

"—happen?" Rani shook her head. "Nothing bad. Queen Ree picked fairies to get Kyto's hoard."

"How will . . ." Gwendolyn stopped herself. She'd been about to ask how they would carry everything. Never underestimate a fairy. They would do it.

What will be in the hoard? she wondered. Gold? Silver? Jewels?

"Are you . . ." She stopped again, before asking if they were going to form the metal things in his hoard into new pots and pans and bedsprings and shovels and everything else. "You're going to give him his whole hoard, aren't you?"

"It's his," Rani said, as if there weren't any other considerations.

Kyto has improved his situation, Gwendolyn thought. He was a captive again but no longer cooped up in a cave. His hoard was being delivered to him, and—knowing fairies—everything in it would be cleaned and repaired, if repairs were needed, and cunningly arranged for his pleasure. So, he had more space. He would have his treasures. And he had a friend—Vidia.

It didn't seem fair.

Yet . . . It might not be fair that she, Gwendolyn, could see and hear fairies again after kidnapping six of them. Maybe neither was fair but both were kind.

She gathered her courage for the question she dreaded. "How . . ." She swallowed. "How . . ." Say it! "How many fairies—"

"—died?" Rani mopped her tears with a leafkerchief. "Seven." She sobbed.

Seven! Gwendolyn's eyes filled. "The flutist. Who else?"

Prilla wiped her eyes on the hem of Gwendolyn's skirt. "Faye and Carlotta . . . They were scouts."

Gwendolyn hiccupped, tears streaming.

Rani choked out, "The sparrow man Quince and Lilla . . ."

Prilla hiccupped too and said, "Grenni and Yvet, fast fliers. Twelve more were injured, but—"

"—they're fine now."

Gwendolyn put her head in her hands. Seven talent members, seven personalities, seven irreplaceable fairies. Their rooms in the Home Tree would be empty. Fairy Haven would be poorer without them.

Gradually her hiccups died down, but she and the two fairies continued crying. Finally Prilla and Gwendolyn dried their eyes. Rani went on weeping.

"I thought he was going to kill everyone. I thought . . ." Gwendolyn hiccupped again. ". . . there would be no more fairies except Vidia. After I left . . ." She took a deep breath. "What kept him from crisping all of you?"

"The water birds." Rani laughed in the middle of her tears. "He hated them."

Prilla laughed too. "He yelled at them and called them 'water—'"

"'—vultures.'" Rani's tears seemed half happy now. "'Fake fliers,' 'fire killers.'"

Prilla turned a cartwheel. "We got better at dodging his flame, too."

Strengths Kyto couldn't guess at.

I didn't have to guess, Gwendolyn thought ruefully. I'd been told. I'd seen what fairies could do with the dragon suit and Tink's Kyto Keeper, but I didn't believe.

Believing would have been part of being *beware*. She'd failed until the very end, and even then *bewareness* hadn't helped. Working out puzzles had helped—her real talent.

Prilla added, laughing, "And the musicians and singers made so much noise they threw his aim off."

Gwendolyn nodded. Of course they would. She asked the other question that had been itching at her. "How long has it been since I grabbed Vidia?"

Prilla said, "Four—"

"—days until you woke up the first time. Five days now."

Five! Gwendolyn gulped. So this was the morning of her last day on Never Land.

Dulcie flew to her with a nut-and-raisin roll, which had finally gone stale.

"Delicious."

"That's what everyone says, but I know better. Since when are fairies polite?"

"I'm not a fairy."

"Same difference," Dulcie said.

Same difference between her and a fairy? "Really?" Gwendolyn jumped up and turned a somersault worthy of Prilla. "Same difference!"

Prilla laughed. "A fairy-snatching-talent Clumsy."

Gwendolyn blushed. That wasn't a good talent.

"No," Rani said. "A dragon-scaring-talent Clumsy."

Gwendolyn liked that one much better.

Tink must have finished her chat with the boulder, because she and Terence flew over. When they drew close, she saw they were carrying a lump of blackened metal between

them. Instantly she knew what it was—her kiss.

"I'd fly backwards if I could," Tink said as she and Terence placed it in Gwendolyn's hand.

"It isn't your fault." The lump felt cold and used up.

Terence landed on the ground by Gwendolyn's left sneaker. Tink perched on her shoulder.

"I can shape the silver the way it used to be and polish it, but the acorn button"—Tink shrugged apologetically—"is a cinder."

Gwendolyn held out the kiss remains. "Make a stew pot."

Terence flew up to help hold it.

Tink smiled. "It wants to be a cake pan and a cookie sheet and a muffin tin."

"Fine."

"Can I have them?" Dulcie asked.

"Can she?" Tink said.

Gwendolyn nodded. Then, wanting to change the subject, she asked, "Why is Kyto inspecting the chain?"

Terence grinned. "He's admiring his reflection."

Tink said, "He keeps twisting the chain to see himself at a different angle. I heard him say . . ." She laughed. "'My snout is *not* too short.'"

"He'll never get free." Terence looked proudly at Tink, whose glow blushed. "Tink says the iron in the boulder is growing into the iron in the earth."

The quest had succeeded. The island had been rescued. Gwendolyn said, "I have to leave today."

Prilla said, "You should stay. I wish you would."

Oh, those words! Gwendolyn wished she could stay—and be at home with Mother and Father and Grandma. She wished she could zip back and forth, like Prilla. She burst out, "Prilla? Will you blink over for a visit sometimes?"

Prilla tweaked her ear. "Yes! Often. But I can never stay long."

Gwendolyn nodded. Even short visits would be wonderful.

Tink tugged her bangs and, wonder of wonders, a tear slid down her nose. Terence wiped his eyes. Rani's leafkerchief was soaked.

Gwendolyn didn't want to leave on sadness. She breathed deeply and waited until the urge to cry faded.

Of course she had to say good-bye to Queen Ree and Beck and especially Mother Dove. She shouldered her backpack, which felt oddly heavy, and flew to the nest. Every single fairy came too, even Vidia.

Gwendolyn crouched. "Mother Dove . . ."

Queen Ree sniffled.

"Mother Dove . . . I tried to learn to *beware*, but I didn't." She shrugged, recognizing the truth. "I don't think I can. I'm a clumsy Clumsy, a jump-in-with-both-feet Clumsy."

"Gwen-n-n-dol-l-l-yn-n-n, we're lucky you didn't leave when I told you to."

"Thank— Er. Thank you." Gwendolyn would miss Mother Dove's coos and her wisdom almost as much as she'd miss fairies. "Thank you for helping to put out my fire."

Mother Dove cooed.

"Mother Dove . . ." Gwendolyn placed a hand on the ground for balance. "Do you think . . . Will I go on seeing fairies when I grow up? When Prilla blinks over, will I always be able to see and hear her?"

"Gwen-n-n-dol-l-l-yn-n-n, perhaps. Never Land will decide. I can't tell it what to do."

Gwendolyn nodded and stood up. A minute or two passed. No one seemed to want to say the final *Fly with you.*

"Darling, this is tiresome." Vidia soared back to Kyto.

"Sweet," she called, "can I ride on your breath?" She hovered in front of his snout.

He looked up from the Kyto Keeper chain. "Yes, quicksilver." He blew a stream of smoke.

Vidia sailed past everyone, screaming her delight.

"Open your backpack," Dulcie said.

Gwendolyn pulled it off. It was full of stale raisin-nut rolls.

"You'll need to eat on your way home."

"Thank—" Gwendolyn nodded. "It was kind of you."

"Eat one when you get hungry. Or sleepy. It will help you stay awake."

She would save one and have a remembrance until it crumbled. A roll baked by Dulcie would likely have long staying-together power.

"Under the rolls," Terence said, "are sacks of fairy dust, enough to get you here again if Peter forgets to come."

This was the best possible gift. Gwendolyn smiled and blinked away fresh tears. "I'll be back as soon as Mother and Father and Grandma let me."

Queen Ree pronounced her quest words. "Be careful, Gwendolyn. Be kind. Be a Clumsy at her best."

Terence poured a fresh sack of fairy dust over her. She began to fly.

THIRTY-TWO

GWENDOLYN didn't stop at Fairy Haven. Fast fliers had already told the fairies there that all was well. But she did visit the underground home where she informed Peter that he didn't have to fly her to the mainland.

"I know the way," she said. "In the day I head for the rising sun. At night I steer away from the star named Peter."

He nodded, then cocked his head. "The mainland is close just now. You will have a short flight, Wendy."

"Gwendolyn. Before I leave . . ." She sat—hovered, really—just above the surface of the bed.

The Lost Boys sprawled around her. Peter stood in front of his tree.

She recited a dozen fairy tales, picking stories they probably hadn't heard before: one about a dwarf who loved to cook; one about a girl in toad form who could make a tiny dog come out of a walnut shell; and another, everyone's favorite, about a boy who rode a horse up a hill made of glass.

Finally she stood. "Good-bye. My parents are expecting me."

Peter said, "Where is your kiss?"

Gwendolyn hiccupped. "I lost it."

"I see." He hopped on one foot. "Too bad then."

"Yes." She rose up the tree that had been whittled for her.

She spent one night over the ocean, but Dulcie's rolls kept her awake. The following night, just after sunset, she flew in her bedroom window at Number 14, where Mother and Father and Grandma were waiting.

A month later, Prilla blinked into Number 14 and landed on the jigsaw puzzle Gwendolyn was putting together. Filling Prilla's arms was a canvas sack. She set it down and turned cartwheels on the puzzle, laughing and laughing, until every piece had scattered.

"Open the sack. It's from Tink."

Gwendolyn's big fingers could hardly untie the triple knot, and trembling didn't help. While she worked at it, she asked, "Did she fix her unleaky colander?"

"It went into Kyto's collar, but now she's repairing a pot that turns whatever is put in it into cherry pits."

The knot came loose at last. Gwendolyn drew out a silver chain as thin as thread, but with a clasp big enough for Clumsy fingers to manage.

On the chain, roughly the size of the old kiss, was a silver frying pan.

"Turn it over," Prilla said.

Etched across the entire back was Tink's talent mark, a pot with steam rising and the letters *TB*.

Oh, my! "It's beautiful."

"The silver comes from pirate treasure. It's the same silver as Queen Ree's new tiara. Tink said to do this when you hiccup . . ." Prilla guided Gwendolyn's hand around the frying pan.

"I will."

Prilla had to leave. "Fly with you," she said and was gone.

Gwendolyn said to the air where she'd been, "Fly with you." Then she added what Clumsies say, "Thank you."

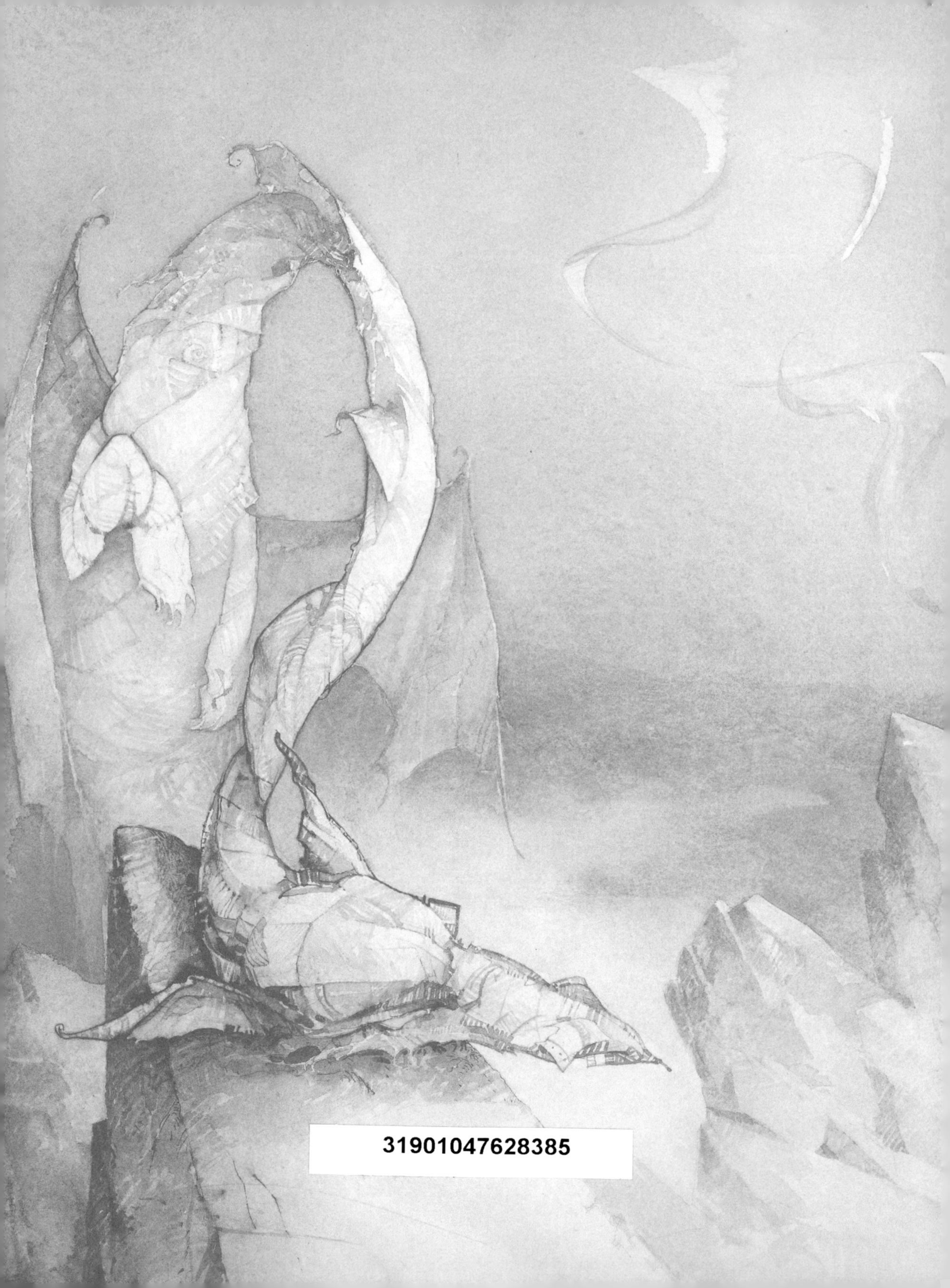